Harvest
& Song for My Time

Stories by
Meridel Le Sueur

West End Press &
MEP Publications
Minneapolis

The writings in this volume first appeared as follows:

"Harvest," unpublished ms., 1929; *West End* Magazine, Fall 1977.
"Fudge," *Fantasy*, Winter 1933.
"Autumnal Village," *Drafts*, Oct.-Nov. 1940.
"God Made Little Apples," *Prairie Schooner*, Winter 1942.
"To Hell with You, Mr. Blue!" *Fantasy*, 1941.
"We'll Make Your Bed," *New Masses*, May 7, 1946.

"Song for My Time," *Mainstream*, Winter 1947.
"Eroded Woman," *Masses and Mainstream*, Sept. 1948.
"Summer Idyl," *Masses and Mainstream*, Sept. 1949.
"American Bus," *Masses and Mainstream*, April 1953.
"Of this Time, upon this Earth," *Masses and Mainstream*, Nov. 1954.
"The Dark of the Time," *Masses and Mainstream*, Aug. 1956.
"The Return of Lazarus," with Elmer Borman, *Mainstream*, June 1958.

*Photo: Children with Pumpkins, by Kenneth Wright
Courtesy Minnesota State Historical Society*

This edition is copublished by:

West End Press
Box 7232
Minneapolis, MN 55407

ISBN 0-931122-27-9

MEP Publications
c/o Dept. of Anthropology
University of Minnesota
215 Ford Hall, 224 Church St. S.E.
Minneapolis, MN 55455
ISBN 0-930656-29-6 (cloth)
ISBN 0-930656-30-x (pap)

Printed in the United States of America

Table of Contents

Harvest

Song for My Time

Dedicated to
Rachel and Kenneth
for haven and love

and

For John Crawford—
more than editor,
excavator, illuminator and discoverer

Foreword

These stories represent the best work of Meridel Le Sueur from two distinct periods: 1929-1946, during which she gained access to the major literary journals and magazines, and 1947-1958, during which she was blacklisted and her works were printed only in the radical press.

Daughter of the pioneer midwestern educator Marian Wharton, stepdaughter of the socialist Arthur Le Sueur, Meridel drew her early inspiration from such diverse sources as the Industrial Workers of the World and the Communist Party, the Hollywood movie industry of the twenties, Bohemian writers' enclaves in Chicago and Greenwich Village, and the Writers Congresses of the thirties. Her work was saluted by the literary geniuses of the day, including Willa Cather, Carl Sandburg, Theodore Dreiser, Sherwood Anderson, Sinclair Lewis, and Nelson Algren. Later, she wrote for *New Masses, Masses and Mainstream*, the *Daily Worker* and other Movement publications.

The first six stories of the present collection, previously printed in West End's 1977 *Harvest*, are written for the general literary audience of the thirties. None are collected elsewhere. The remaining stories, from West End's 1977 *Song for My Time*, present a stunning view of the United States in the era following the Second World War. Of these seven stories, five are unique to this collection.

Meridel Le Sueur is no longer, in 1982, in need of "rediscovery." International Publishers kept her work in print during the darkest times, and West End's volumes helped those engaged in recent struggles to heed the voices of the "other America." Most recently, the Feminist Press selection bears witness to the role played by the new Women's Movement in creating a new audience.

The energy of Meridel herself is unflagging. "We want all to march," she wrote in the thirties; for the Bicentennial she announced "Survival is a form of resistance" and prophesied "choruses of millions/singing." She has never stopped marching, surviving, singing, and inspiring others to join her. It is appropriate that our part in keeping the connection open between this people's artist and her public now be shared. With the copublication of this collection of stories and the simultaneous reissue of her novel *The Girl*, we address her with her own words:

> We pledge to you our guerrilla
> fight against the predators of our country.

John Crawford, West End Press
Doris Grieser Marquit, MEP Publications
Minneapolis, September 1982

Harvest

It was almost noon and the sun stood hot above the fields. The men would be coming in from the corn for dinner.

Ruth Winji stooped at the bean vines thinking she had not enough yet in her basket for a mess of beans. From the hour's picking of berries and beans she had leaned over in her own heat and the sun's heat driving through her until earth memory and seed memory were in her in the hot air and she was aware of all that stood in the heat around her, the trees in the bright sun, earth-rooted, swaying in sensitive darkness, the wheat like a sea in the slight wind, the cows peering from the caverns of shade of the grove behind the barns with their magic faces and curved horns. Root darkness. Tree darkness. Sun. Earth. Body. She thought: *And my body dark in the sun, root-alive, opening in the sun dark at its deep roots*, and it pained her now that she had quarrelled with her husband.

Anxiously she lifted her large fair torso looking for her young husband as he would come from the corn and wheat, swaying a little as he walked, the sun flashing up the stalk of his body, trying not to show the joy he had walking toward her. By noon she always looked to see him come back, for they had not been separated longer in the six months of their marriage. She shaded her face to see him but she could not tell him at that distance from the other two men that worked in the corn. Still she looked trying to find out what he would be doing for she grieved that a quarrel stood up between them, and now she could not tell him that they would have a child.

It was a quarrel about whether he should buy a threshing machine to harvest the ripening wheat. It wasn't that the money was her dowry money; she dreaded the machine. She knew how men came in from riding that monster all day. She had been hired out before her marriage in the three years since she had come from Bohemia and she knew the cold mindless look of them, not in a column of mounting heat as her husband came now to her, a flame from the earth, broken off as if the quick of it had taken to his very flesh.

Her heart went into a great dismay to think of him riding that machine, and she saw with what a glitter that desire sat upon him and her heart was sick. He had never had a machine and now he wanted one, and it was an encroachment like another woman or war.

She leaned over again thrusting her hand in to the warm vine foliage as the berries hung turning away from the heat upon themselves and she plucked them from the short thick stems and they fell sun-heavy in her hand. Her fingers were stained with berry juice and it had run up the naked belly of her arm and dried there.

She could not keep her mind from thinking how more and more now he looked into that catalogue at night where there were pictures shown of all the parts of a thresher. How he looked into this book all the evening without speaking a word.

Their marriage had been wonderful to her in mid-winter. Coming to his farm, snowed in together in January, and it was as if they themselves brought the spring, warming spreading it from their own bodies until it lifted and mounted from the house to the fields, until the whole earth was jutting in green.

Then she had come with him while he plowed and planted or watched him from the windows of the house as if he stood still in union with her as he strode the sun-scarred earth laying it open, the seed falling in the shadows; then at evening he came from them to her, himself half young, half old in the beginnings of his body, his young brows aslant meeting above his nose, his lips full and red, the sun warming and jutting in him too as the spring advanced, and she was not loath to accept him from the fields smelling of salt sweat, and see all that he had planted ripen and grow from that wild heat into the visible world, bright and green, rising to its flower, and now a child growing unseen but certain.

Still and even now, the knowing and remembering in herself of the way of his walking or the manner of his speech, as if he were out of breath, coming partly from the newness of the language to him and partly from his eagerness to know everything, his terrible cunning to know: That was it, that was what she really feared, his new world cunning to know, that's what made the fear go up her body so she had to lift her heavy shoulders and breathe slowly looking out over the slow sheen of the turning wheat where everything seemed almost dark in the sun. Still she could not see him, only the three tiny figures of the hoeing men far afield in the corn.

Now she felt she was losing him, as if he were falling out of some soft burr, their ancient closed fertile life, being shaken from the old world tree, in ways beyond her, that she would not go.

The days in the early spring had been like great hot needles sewing them close together, in and out, binding them close, piercing through both to the marrow and binding them with the bright day and the dark night. So the earth lay and herself too, marked by the plow. The sun rose molten with intent. The sun went down and the dusk blew scented and low upon them. The light of day spun them together in utter tranquility — until he had to come saying, "What about this machine? They say that the work will be done so quick, you wouldn't believe it. They say it, Ruth. What about it? We have just enough to have it. What about it?"

And it was just as if he were about to betray her and she could say nothing, seeing that look of greed and cunning, and it was no good to argue this or that because everyone threshed his wheat with the big harvester and he would get her to peek into the catalogue and tell her how the thing mowed the wheat in terrible broad swaths and he showed her the picture of the seat where he would sit swaying sensitive in his own rich body from that iron seat and then she wouldn't look. She would turn away in fear and it came to lie heavier in her than her own planting that she bore now to the fourth month.

And he kept saying, "We could get one of those, Ruth. We could save money. We could just get one of those." With his curious way of repeating himself, beginning and ending on the same phrase. "I was over there looking at that machine in town. Pretty good, too. Yah, pretty good. I was over there looking and it was good." At those times she wouldn't know him at all, that sensual light would be gone from his young keen face, the little flicker that came up from his body gone, and he would be smiling, distracted, rubbing his palms together, as if he were falling away from her, out of the column of himself to be lost to her touch.

The salesman had even come and Winji had looked askance, speaking low so the man left quickly and she took it as a good sign.

She saw the sun topping the roof of the barn so she hurried up the lane with her berries and her beans. Then she heard a sound that made her step in fright. She saw that monster coming slowly up the road making a corrugated track. It came as if with no motion of its parts through the heat. Ruth Winji ran into the cooled house, closed the door then stood hearing that beat that was like a heart and yet monstrous. It seemed to be going straight over the house and she didn't look out until it had passed and then she saw the monstrous tracks on the road bed.

She remembered her husband had said they were demonstrating one at Olson's and had wanted her to go with him to see and she had said she would not go.

She put the beans on and sat down to wait at the window where she could first see him come up through the orchard. The sunlight made an under-darkness over the lower world so it was dark as a plum, the trees still black-tipped, a sensitive shimmer of darkness like a convulsion seemed to go over the sun or world beneath the gloom of sun so Ruth went into a swoon of heat between the bright upper sun and the painfully sensitive lower darkness.

She must have dozed because she started aware when her husband stood in the room behind her. She didn't turn from the window but knew him there in the soft heated gloom. He hadn't spoken behind her in the room and her body started alive to him like a blind antenna upreaching. He touched her shoulder coming from behind her and she saw his hands burned rosy. She thrust back against him and he still stood invisible touching her.

There was a drowsiness of noon all about them, the soft throaty cluck of the hens, the padding of the dog across the bare swept ground, the crisp whirr of a bird startled up from noon drowse winging from shadow to shadow.

She looked up, saw his face, young, dark, mounted with blood rosy beneath the burned skin, his brows winged strangely at an angle as she looked up, his full young mouth curved willfully, his eyes glinting above her like the eyes of a hawk looking at her from his narrow spare face coming down on her from above, setting his lips on hers.

"The beans," she cried.

"Never mind," he said enamored, "I turned the fire off. Never mind."

Her springing up as she had lifted his whole height to her instantly like a shaft of shadow against the bright outdoors light. Seeing the straight willful neck, plunging to the close-cropped round head, springing against his hard spare sweating body, she pinned him with her arms where the shirt was set and stuck to his strong back and felt the winging of the ribs' spare flight, spanning from her hands the hard thin breast.

At table Winji talked with the hired help about the thresher that had gone by. Ruth listened with lowered head.

"My wife here," Winji said, "doesn't want me to buy it. She wants to keep the old way, God knows why."

The other two men looked at her, the full confused woman sitting at table with them. They seemed to hardly dare lay eyes upon her.

"Well, it's a good one for getting work done," said one.

And they went on talking about threshers and their good and bad points and their makes like man enamoured until she said, "Don't talk about it please, don't speak."

"But we will," her husband said leaning towards her, his fork upraised. "And you're going down with me after this meal and see how it goes."

She did not dispute with him before the men.

After the dishes were cleared he said in the kitchen, "Listen Ruth. The thresher is just down the bend. That's the one I've been talking about. Listen Ruth. I wish you would go down there with me."

"No," she said, wiping off the dishpan carefully.

"You go down and look at it with me. I think it's the best thing we should do. Get it. Buy it. You go down, just for my sake."

"No," she said. "No, I don't want to see it. I'm afraid."

He laughed sharply, his white teeth frightening in his red mouth. "Oh, you'll think it's wonderful when you get over that. Why, it's wonderful."

"No," she said. "It's not wonderful to me."

"Think of it," he said, his eyes glistening in that way she had seen, beyond desire for her. "It will bind the sheaves after it has cut the wheat. . . ."

"What," she said, "bind the sheaves. . . ."

"Yes," he nodded and she saw that lust for knowing and what she took for cunning. "Bind the sheaves at the same time."

"At the same time," she repeated stupidly, "without going around again."

"Yes," he almost shouted, "without going around again."

"Think, how many men did it take on your father's place in the old country to harvest the wheat . . ."

"Yes. . . . Yes, I know," she said, wringing her hands. "I used to carry a brown jug to the men full of spring water with a little meal sprinkled in it. . . ."

"You just sit on the machine and pull levers, see. Like this." He sat down and pulled levers with nothing in his hands.

"How do you know how?" she said. "You've been practicing," she cried.

"What of it," he said like a boy, as if he had got hold of something. "What if I have. Come with me, Ruth. It's your money in a way . . ."

"No, no," she said. "It's your money. Do with it as you like. It's yours. You're the master of the house, but don't make me see it. I don't want to see it. I wash my hands. I wash my hands . . . "

He stood grinning, shaking his head, chagrined a little: "But you can't wash your hands of the whole new world . . ."

But nevertheless she cried after him from the kitchen, "No. No, I wash my hands," and he went out slowly from her, bewildered.

In an hour she went with him, prevailed upon by his physical power over her. He took her hand in the road and pulled her along. Her face was partly covered by her blue sun bonnet and she hid the free hand under her apron. When they got there a clot of men gathered over the machine like black bees and she stood back. Winji joined them, hardly concealing his delight, going time and again round and round the machine. It was brand new and glinted monstrously in the light.

"Look Ruth, look," he kept saying to her, running back and pointing things out and then running back to the machine. "Look at this," he would say but she couldn't hear. She watched his face in envy and malice. The other men were laughing at her but she didn't care.

"No, no," she kept saying, half-obscured in her sun bonnet, pulling away as her husband tried to urge her to look closer at the thresher. The other men looked at her full woman's body, awed a little and thinking how the two were so newly married. They stood away from her a little sheep-faced and she stood away from them and the machine.

"Come and touch it," Winji urged.

"No, no," she cried, "I don't want to."

"Why, it won't hurt you," the men said. "Don't be afraid."

She could see her husband was a bit ashamed of her, and chagrined. "You know," he said to the men, apologizing for her, "in the old country we don't have them like this, in the old country . . ."

She saw the men patting him on the back as if he had already bought the thresher, envy showing in their eyes and he grew big from their envy, strutting around the machine, rubbing his palms together, forgetting her for a moment so she went cold with dread, then running to her to propitiate her.

"Come and touch it, isn't it splendid, look at that." She saw the big knives thrusting back movement even in their stillness, and then on driving power and the tiny man-seat hidden inside, where the little living man was supposed to sit and pull the levers as her husband had been showing her. She was revolted.

But he came close to her and she was bewitched still of his body so she let herself be led straight to the giant and saw all its shining steel close to her and her husband took her hand, still stained by berries, and put it on the steel rump and it was hot as fire to the touch so she drew back nursing her hand. The men laughed and her eyes dilated holding to her husband's face but drawing away.

The men were uneasy. "Never mind, Winji," they said, "lots of our women folks takes it that way at first. My wife says her house was buried in dust the first year the thresher come." They laughed uneasily, shifting, and looking from under their brows at the woman. They turned with ease back to the machine.

She started away down the road. At the bend she turned and looked back and to her horror she saw her husband caressing the great steel body. He was dancing, a little quick dance full of desire, and with his quick living hands he was caressing the bright steel where the sun struck and flew off shining from the steel rumps into her eyes like steel splinters so she turned back sickened, but not before she saw him wave to her, a shy lifting of the hand.

She hadn't told him she was going to have a child. She thought of the child now as a weapon.

She waited while the tension went tighter between them subtly, unspoken now, with his saying now and then at breakfast, at dinner, "Have you changed? What have you against it? Is it a beast?"

She wouldn't answer, only turned against him. And then he turned against her, chagrined and lost without her, trying to win her back to his way and she wouldn't come.

She would cajole him, sitting on his lap in the evening when it was too hot to sleep. "Don't do it. Don't get it." But he knew she was playing a trick to get him. Once he got up, setting her on her own feet and walking away, and that night he didn't come in until late and didn't speak to her but went soundly to sleep.

He grew subtle against her, his summer face hot and congealed, his straight burned neck a pillar of blood against her, his brooding body hot from labor, a wall to her now that made her blind and angered.

When he came in from the cattle with the beast smell about him and milk on his shoes and the lustre of living things, she tried to pull him to her again.

At last there was enmity between them. He didn't talk any more about the machine. They sat together at table without speaking and went to bed silently in the late dusk and she thought he would never come to her again. She felt he was betraying all that and her grief was bitter against a new way, terrible in her so she didn't tell him about the child.

Then one day she went to town and came back early to be near him and go on with the fight, to bring it to come, and there she saw the salesman and Winji at the table leaning over the catalogue and figures and before they shut the book she could see the knives and parts of the machine in color. The two men looked at her guiltily. Winji got up and walked with his back to her and stood stock still at the window. The salesman left as quickly as possible and the two of them stood in the room.

"So!" she said bitterly. "You are going to get it."

"Yes!" he said and she could see the blood flush up his bared neck. "Yes, I am."

"So you don't care," she said, shaking bitterly, clenching her hands together, for she could have torn him to pieces standing there presenting his back to her. "You don't care," she said.

"I don't know what that means." Still he didn't face her. He seemed a stranger with his back turned. "It's for our good to get the machine. This is just woman's stubbornness. It will get us on. We will be powerful people in this neighborhood. . . ."

"Powerful . . ." she repeated.

"Yes," he said now, turning to her uneasily but against her.

She began to cry, not lifting her hands.

The sight of her exasperated him. "What are you crying for," he said in real anger but his face looked guilty. "What are you crying for," he shouted, raising his hand. "Stop that bellowing," he swore and struck her.

She recoiled, her face lifted wide to his. He saw her falling back, her great eyes open upon him in grief. He gave a cry and caught her falling arms, thrust her toward himself. Against her he stood straight and she began to cry from her body shaking, rent by the grief in her. He held her and for a moment seemed to know what she had been feeling but it was only for a moment.

Then it was she told him about the child.

He seemed to forget about the machine those long summer days and everything was as it had been before. She looked at him every day and it seemed that it was over. He was bound to her again and she was content.

The wheat hung heavy on the stalk.

She thought he had arranged to have the old red reaper of Olson's and hire many men and she had already spoken for two of the girls to come in and help feed since she was slower on her feet now too.

One day he came in in the early afternoon and she saw he was excited.

He prowled around the house all afternoon and she was uneasy. "Is anything the matter?" she asked him. "No," he said. But when she wasn't looking she caught him looking at her. At supper he said nervously, as if he had been preparing for it the whole afternoon:

"Tomorrow we begin." He kept looking at his coffee but he kept smiling and looking cunningly at her when she wasn't looking.

"Tomorrow?"

"Huh," he grunted.

She set down her knife and fork, unable to eat. "Well?" she said, a cold fear making her hollow.

"I've got a surprise for you," he said.

"A surprise," she said.

"Don't repeat what I say!" he suddenly shouted, threw down his spoon and left the table.

The next morning she woke sitting bolt upright and saw his place beside her empty. She ran to the window but it was just dawn and she could see nothing. She dressed and put on the coffee. Still he did not come. Suddenly she put on a sweater and went as fast as she could down the lane to the beanfield where she could see the wheat and there in the field she saw it standing new and terrible, gleaming amidst the sea of ripe wheat that crested and foamed gently to its steel prow and receded away in heavy fruition.

It was over. There it was. She couldn't say why she was so afraid but she knew it was against her and against him. It was a new way.

A bevy of men stood around. Then they saw her and Winji left them and came towards her beckoning, but she did not move towards him. He came to her.

"Don't be angry, Ruth," he said gently. "We've got to do it." We can't be behind the times, can we? Now with the child."

"No," she said. They both knew that the clot of men around the machine were half-looking their way, waiting to see what would happen.

"Isn't she a beauty," he said in his broken tongue.

"A beauty," she said.

"For God's sake, do you have to repeat after me for God's sake," he said, then beseeching, he begged of her for the first time. "You say it's all right, darling. Ruth, you say it's all right. We've got to get ahead, you know that. Now more than ever, haven't we?" he said softly, standing only a foot away, but she felt his spell.

"Yes, yes," she said in grief, "yes. . . ."

"Go on," she said. "Go on with it."

"But you come down to the fence and see me go down the field the first time," he begged.

She hated him but she went behind him, seeing his heels flicker up as he went in haste, eager to be with his new "beauty."

The mare in the pasture came up and walked near him and stood sadly with them at the fence whinnying softly as her master went down the field, letting the air tremble through her soft nostrils.

Walking away he heard the soft bleat of the mare, felt the men waiting from the machine and for a moment a kind of fear struck him through the marrow as he saw the glistening thing standing to his hand. Down his soft loins, his vulnerable breast, went a doom of fear and yet an awful pride, but he felt shaking at the bones, for leaving the moistness of sleep, the old world of close dreaming in the thick blossomed surface, and the space of mystery where the seed unfolds to the touch in the cool and thick and heavy sap, the world of close dreaming that is like a woman's hair or the breasts of men.

She saw him turn in the sun — wave to her and mount the machine.

Fudge

I heard the story bit by bit, piecing it together and watching Nina Shelley as she moved to her windows, spying back upon the Town that had set her like a fly in amber, hardening in her own and their hatred.

I saw her too when she came to church and how there was a hush and a withdrawing from her, for she was a visible sign of their own lust and had now come into the Town's dreams, with her urgency that had lasted so short a time. They congealed and flowed around her in their bitterness, she, being sign and symbol, set up for all to see on church day and on market day, coming gruesomely for food for spirit and for body, to feed the corpse they had already buried for her. The women never embraced or touched her, and held her off from their children, from their own warm hearths, glad that she, by her sparsity, made their own bitterness seem abundant and rich.

She was always phoning, asking young girls or young school teachers to come over and see her. Not many would go. Some went out of curiosity and perhaps out of sympathy. Then they told what had been said and what had happened. They always made fudge for one thing and sometimes sang hymns and looked at the pictures of Nina Shelley's dead mother and father and cousins and aunts and uncles who never came to see her now but sent her a little money at Christmas. She still did the same things she had been doing when *it* had happened, the things young girls and school teachers used to do.

So I wasn't surprised when she phoned me. Standing on tip-toe in the hall where I could look right across the street and see her house, I heard her voice and felt in it all that had happened to her uncoil and spring out of the darkness, as if it rang still in the body of that disaster.

"Hello, yes, Miss Shelley," I was a young girl then and took upon myself all that had happened to her as a possible thing that might happen to me when things began to happen, and as a thing that would be better than nothing happening at all.

"Hello, hello, talk louder, dearie," said the voice. "This is Miss Shelley. I'm making some candy this afternoon, and I saw you kind of lonesome-like in the yard and thought, well, I'll call her up and ask her to come over this afternoon and we'll make some candy. All right, dearie, all right.''

I could look right across the street and see her house that looked as if it did not enfold or enshrine, but carried a burden it could not name, written on all the low wooden gables, the glassy windows like a sneer and a grimace. Every time I looked I had to taste that evil, bitterly, like some old thing rotting in the house, giving out a smell until everything became musty of it, letting out more of a being in decay than its wholeness ever had.

There were many in the Town who thought they knew about that moment when something had happened and then stopped happening to Miss Shelley, so she had to spit upon all that was in the Town and look askance at what was growing, putting upon it an evil and a disillusionment. People carried cunning pieces of that design of what had happened; and the worst of it was, she never knew who carried which piece. And she herself became lost in the confusion of what had happened and the myth and dream that had grown in herself mixed with the things people made up about it. So after a time it seemed that every person had a part of the design distorted and shaped to his or her own image.

What had happened I imagine had been more than the Town could imagine and less than they rolled so glibly on their tongues. I felt myself, looking at it from the point of being a young girl, a little younger than Miss Shelley herself had been when it had happened to her, that possibly she had only tried once to step out of herself and that time had curdled and embittered her. So she peered out now with malice, seeing the doings of the Town, knowing them all to be on the way to death and believing not one thing was let off from that curse. Malice then would be the cover of pity in her for what she knew to be in the world, and unwittingly she would pass on to the young girls who came to her the thing that had defiled her, having nothing in her hands but that defilement.

With intricate care, feeling it was a thing could happen to any young girl, I put the pieces together one person saying one thing, another adding to the pattern a bitter bit, another taking that away.

When Miss Shelley had been a girl with puffed sleeves, and an eye out like any other for what could be for her, she hadn't wanted more than to touch, to be made to move like wind and fire with grace toward what might be rich.

I thought that when she had been a young girl that she might have stood in front of her mirror as I stood, letting down her hair, waiting for that fulfillment, as I waited too, and all the time walking amidst the malice that stood ready to ensnare her, and the defeat that was bred more deeply than she knew. Perhaps she had been full of terror, as I was too, seeing that what stood up in her dreams had no reality in the lives of the Town, and imagining, as I imagined too, that there might be some sin that would make her life fettered and barren; yet examining what was in her she must have found, as I did, that there was only goodness in her ways.

Then it must have come upon her swift as a fire I once saw consume a child, leaping to the skirts and quicker than movement, lick, grow upon what it fed, until the hair stood on end, aflame. From the moment that summer when she had first seen Watson Hawk, standing on the church steps, his wild face had fled down her blood, to be there all her life. When he would not have known her on the street, or standing up amongst old ladies in a parlor, his face would be plunging through her, a knife cutting her down.

I knew how she must have looked his way at the band concerts, amidst the circling summer dresses of girls walking arm in arm, swishing on, looking back. And she had to follow him, being drawn, going down the streets of the Town on summer nights looking for his face, asking for that doom until all the men in front of the livery stable were laughing, winking as she passed, slapping their thighs, seeing that strained girl's face looking for Hawk, asking it of him, watching and glad to see her come upon this snare, seeing that she would be entrapped as they had been, and would be one of them.

The Town had wrapped itself warmly in what had happened after that. There were many tales. What had it been? The tongues clacked, striking flint on flint. After Hawk shot her or she shot herself, the carriages had driven slowly past the Shelley house, peering at every stick to find it out, to taste what had happened, what had been known. And even to this day I peered at every doorway of that house and at every bone and piece of skin of Nina Shelley as if they would give up that secret at last and it could be spoken for her and for us all.

Like a pack of starved wolves they fed on her then and after until she wore as thin as a bone.

After they brought her back where she had been found lying in that shed beside the railroad, people had gotten shreds of it all in their teeth worrying it to find what each part belonged to and what the meaning could be.

As well as I could find out, it seems that she had followed Hawk after something had or had not happened between them one day when she had gone on a buggy ride with him out to Mumser's Orchard. No one knew what had happened then or afterwards. All they really knew was that she followed him to the Fair and then they had gone out in the country with a lunch and then she had been found lying in that shed, with her umbrella and a new hat with a red ribbon on it beside her. Either she had shot herself or Hawk had shot her. Miss Shelley never said what happened. No one had heard her say much about it at all when it came right down to it.

Everyone would tell you about how her jacket was lying south of her head, that she had only her last petticoat on, that her skirt had been spread on the ground, as if for a bed, that her umbrella, of all things with a hawk's head on it, had been lying west of the cross timber or was it east? near the front of the shed; and had it been blood the engineer had seen from the five-thirty express to Kansas City or had it been that red ribbon on her hat? Some of the women said they had a piece of that red ribbon but I never saw any of it. Some said Miss Shelley had the umbrella and the hat to this day. But she never showed it. I never saw it.

Afterwards, of course, she couldn't get a school anywhere. Even if the tale had not followed her, she carried it like a guilt, like a child she might have gotten, that would never be born out of her, but would die and rot and eat off her until she was dead. Her family had kept her within itself. She had scarcely gone out of the house, until her father and mother died leaving her alone in the house on Maple Street.

So she had taken to living off what happened to other people as best she could. And the Town lived off what had happened to her. Men enjoyed their wives more and their own loss lay in her and the mutilations they gave each other.

And I, a young girl then, the same as she had been before, saw the way it went, beauty having two ways, disaster, then change, one way or another.

The day I went to Nina Shelley's to make fudge she had asked Cora Little, too; and we both went in together and Cora kept giggling and nudging me and I felt embarrassed and opened my eyes wide and looked straight at Miss Shelley as she opened the door a crack showing her bony nose and one eye; and the shadows of the house then reared up behind her as she opened and we came into the musty dark, seeing the empty chairs and the hand–tinted pictures of her dead mother and father on the wall.

We followed her swishing skirts just seeing her walking primly in front of us but I could feel she was excited and when she turned to let us pass her in the doorway into the kitchen, I could see her eyes glinting and her thin discolored hand shook. I wondered why she liked young girls to come there to make fudge of all things.

But the kitchen was clean and bright, the sun coming in from the back yard, and we could see the green grass, and the way we went to school down past the gravel pit. So we felt better.

"Well, here we are," Miss Shelley said, laughing girlishly and looked at us as if she fed off us or was expecting some rare pleasure of us. I had too an impression I remember that she might want to deal us some blow. I remember I thought quite distinctly, she may want to kill us. I was confused but I remember I knew then that she had asked us there for a purpose and that she asked every young girl there for the same purpose. And it was certainly much more than making fudge.

We weren't much good. Cora stood holding her elbows and kind of giggling and I dropped the mixing bowl so Miss Shelley laughed and began mixing herself, talking in a light girlish voice all the time.

It didn't seem long before the fudge was on the stove just beginning to boil. It was quick because none of us was thinking about the fudge. We were waiting for something. Only Miss Shelley knew what it was.

We sat down by the kitchen table to wait for the fudge to boil and Miss Shelley got a cup of cold water ready to test it and set it beside her. The afternoon sun came in the window and struck on Cora, and I could see the golden hairs on her arms which she put on the table still holding her elbows in her hands, and it fell on the dead rats puffed high over the thin hair of Miss Shelley who sat between us and she kept looking first at Cora and then at me in a terrible excitement. And her red tongue kept licking out over her lips as if her tongue was the only thing left in her with blood in it. And then I remember she leaned over, looking quickly at both of us, her tongue going out over her mouth, and said, her eyes glinting up from her dried skin, "My, I seen a sight in this Town during my time. My, I could tell you a mite."

I could see Cora just gripping her arms and looking down and I could see Miss Shelley's hands gripping the sides of the kitchen chair, her body rigid with some kind of vindictive power that came out of her, as vigor or beauty might come from another. "I seen a sight all right," she said, licking her lips.

Then Cora said, clearing her throat twice and speaking huskily, as if out of politeness more than anything, "What have you seen?"

Miss Shelley opened her eyes full upon us so they showed green in the center, "I seen what was happening to everybody in this Town. I know a heap I don't tell. I suppose you've heard a lot about me, some is right and some is wrong. But I know a heap too. I can tell a heap when I want to."

And I heard myself saying, "Why do you have to tell it?" I was frightened.

"Why do I have to tell it?" Miss Shelley kind of lifted her sharp shoulders and said, "Ha," in a way that made it wrench the cords of her neck out and stretch her mouth and dilate her nose. "Ha," she said, "I got plenty on this Town too. I been sittin' here. I got a sight."

Cora was cracking her knuckles. "I better test the fudge," she said half getting up but Miss Shelley said, "You set down. I know to a minute when it's done." And she leaned forward as if she had been waiting for that moment and I saw how no part of her flowed together with any ease, but every articulation held a tension of hate that made it a wonder she was ever taken in any rest and I knew something awful had happened to her and I didn't want to hear what it was. And yet I knew if she started telling it I would have to listen even though I never heard another thing all my life after that. And it would make the taste of everything bitter.

"Why do you have to tell it?" I said and I felt as if I had shouted it out.

"I got my reasons," Miss Shelley said drumming on the table and looking out the window with absolutely blind eyes; and I looked out too where she should have been looking; and then suddenly I knew, as if someone had told

me, that Miss Shelley had not really looked out that
window since the Thing had happened. A chill crept in the
roots of my hair and my feet were dead at the ends of my
legs and my hands sweated and I thought I'd never be able
to live if I heard what had really happened to her and I felt
that I was going to get up and scream right there, "Don't
tell us. Let us alone. Maybe it won't happen to us too. Let
us alone . . . ."

But just then the candy rose, hissing on the fire.

We were sitting in the back yard then waiting for the
fudge to get hard and Miss Shelley was sitting on the
ground like a young coquettish teacher with her legs pulled
up under her skirt and I could see plainly that time on her
when her body was young and long, when she would be sit-
ging looking with pleasure at what was happening at a picnic or a party. I could see her almost like some part of myself but the ruthless sun made her look like a caricature of
that time and that perfection and showed her up like a
rotten piece of wood.

Cora sat on the other side of her still scrooched over
herself as if she thought Miss Shelley was going to hit her in
the stomach and I kept plucking blades of grass and sliding
them through my teeth but I was shaking and my hands
and feet were numb because I knew she was going to tell us
and nothing could stop her.

And sure enough she began: "You know I expect
you've heard people say plenty about me," she said
smoothing down her old dress with her ghastly bony
fingers and looking up at us beneath her brows and smiling
with her bloodless mouth. "You see," she said, "I almost
got married one time."

Cora and I looked at each other.

"Well," Miss Shelley went on bending her head
sideways just as she must have as a girl but now she looked
strange as if one thing slid across another like a film double
exposed. I remember I felt sick and my pity and dread
went over the old woman. "Yes, Miss Shelley," I said.

"Oh, it ain't much," she said raising her hand stiffly.

"I wouldn't think on it," Cora said in a small voice
bending down over her arms and looking at the grass.

"It's this way, girls," Miss Shelley went on and we
looked at her knowing now we must hear what it was and
nothing could keep us from hearing. "You see I don't
speak of it much, I don't think such things should be
spoken of. They're too sacred." She set her lips so they

didn't show at all and looked over our heads. I kept letting
the green blade slide between my lips but I knew my pity
was ready to flow over what we were about to hear and I
waited thinking the least I could do was to let it fall in a
space of quiet and be mute.

"Yes, Miss Shelley," I said again.

"Well," she said unexpectedly, "I feel my life has
been very, very beautiful." She let her head fall to one
side, the big rats shifting on her head. "Very beautiful,"
she said softly, letting her dead voice fall down as if it lay
far below the sunlight like something under an old board.
She spoke like a ghost so the immediate air was still around
her, as if she did not live in our summer, but was echoing
some lost time, like some fermented decaying thing, rising
filling every moment, its fumes usurping the present entirely. "Very beautiful," she said again. Her eyes closed dra-
matically.

Some delicacy made us look away. Cora looked as if
she was trying to forget all about Miss Shelley and what she
was saying but I knew she was listening to every word.

"You see I was engaged to marry Hawk. Yes, he was
a member of one of the best families in town, that's a fact.
Well, we had a lovely courtship. Nobody in this Town can
say different." She waited. The maple shook. Cora and I
were listening thinking of what might happen to us when
something would begin happening.

"Yes, it was one of the most beautiful things. He was
so tender, so courteous. A woman could not want a more
tender courtship, I often say. It was too perfect, yes, I
often said to my mother, too perfect."

I lowered my head remembering what I had heard men
saying, women saying, seeing then in my mind's eye three
things, what had been said about it, what it had become in
Miss Shelley's mind, fusing together, lapping over, and
then there was a terrific thing stood up beside me between
that old woman and myself — *What had really happened?*

I don't remember the words. I know I was sitting
cramped, not daring to move; knowing I was looking upon
something awful, as Miss Shelley, in her lisping voice, now
becoming shadowed so that you might have been fooled
into thinking it was the voice of the young Miss Shelley
before *it* had happened, her eyes lowered in proper
modesty, told how they had decided their love was too
pure, too perfect for this world . . . more like the love of
Christ for the church . . . that was what she said, and that it

must not be spoiled by mundane things into the poor life
they saw all about them, that it must remain that high pure
thing unsullied by passion. "You understand, girls, I
trust," she said as if she were reading from an invisible
book she held in her hand. "You understand, I trust," she
said, looking at the round downy arms of Cora Little and
at my own long hungering body with contempt. She flung
up her neck, hanging in dead pouches and I knew that to
her it was slim and lovely as a swan's, that her lips fouled
by that shadow were once fair and parted and for a
moment we saw the resurrection by this fantasy of her dead
self, as if it could last.

"Well I remember that summer day," she said, her
smile ghastly on her slanting face. "Mr. Hawk came and
we drove right through the Town, a proud couple we were.
I remember the very dress I wore, and the new parasol
papa brought from Kansas City that matched." Cora and
I looked at each other. Could that have been the very
parasol found beside her when she was found shot? "It
was on that day Mr. Hawk proposed to me. I remember it
as if it was yesterday. Yes . . . yes. . . . We stopped down
by the creek. He was a romantic one, you know, and going
down on his knees he says . . ." She stopped.

"Yes, Miss Shelley," I said in agony. I knew then she
must be lying. Cora was smiling evilly behind her hand
and I was afraid Miss Shelley would see it. But she wasn't
seeing anything in *that* afternoon.

"Yes . . . yes . . ." she said, "yes, well I remember it
like it was yesterday. I do for a fact. And I said no. Loving him like I did, girls, I said no because I didn't want
such a love sullied. That's just the word I used, sullied. We
drove back in the gloaming, very slow. It was beautiful. . . ."

Neither of us could look straight at her. There was a
stillness as if Miss Shelley had stepped off into a vacuum
where we could not follow, beyond that afternoon's sun.
She had her head tilted, that idiotic smile was stretching
her lips as if she sat now, her bones showing, the skin
raveled, under that tiny umbrella amidst her ruffles, beside
Hawk that far afternoon. I shivered right in the sun
because it was like some terrible magic that Miss Shelley
had aged and shriveled but still sat preserved like some
body in a tomb, in that afternoon twenty years before
under an absurd umbrella, expecting something to happen.

Then I saw Cora getting up and I saw that grin on her face that nearly everyone had when they talked or thought about Miss Shelley. I knew she was going to say something awful. I didn't want her to say it. 'See if the fudge is ready to eat," I said to her but I couldn't stop her. She flaunted her skirts around her legs that were more developed than mine and made her seem mature.

"What happened to Hawk," she said pulling down her dress over her full bosom that the girls all envied.

"Hawk? My dear," Miss Shelley said like a great lady. "He has become a great financier. Yes, he changed his name," she said quickly. "No one knows it but myself. And once a year I receive a gorgeous present from him. But I trust all this is between only us." She was very gentle now from her imagined world, for an earth lost in sin, unwilling to be saved, doomed to its own sullied evil.

But I wanted to cry out. "But what really happened? What was it? Warn us. Save us. Nobody tells us anything. You all know something and you don't tell us. . . . What people say isn't so. You'll all go to hell if you don't tell . . . if you don't save us from dying too."

But I didn't say it. I didn't know how. And we all got up and went in to look at the fudge which was just for that afternoon. Nobody ate much except Cora who was still smiling as if she knew something and I was afraid she was going to hurt Miss Shelley more, and I kept wanting to really ask her so my throat ached. I couldn't have swallowed the fudge if some one had paid me.

Cora said wickedly, "I've got to go." And she walked out very boldly, her skirts flicking around her legs where they curved out at the calf and it made me feel I would never be able to leave, that I could not get away as if some evil had spun a web around me so I could not move in any direction. We stood at the screen door watching Cora sway her hips down the green lawn; then I saw her stop, turn and beckon to me. I always did everything Cora told me because of the way her legs and bosom went; and so I stood close to her, smelling that perfume she used, and she began to whisper in my ear. At first I couldn't hear. I could see Miss Shelley still standing in the doorway.

Then I heard quite distinctly what Cora was whispering. "Ask Miss Shelley," she said, "if it was her loving suitor shot her!" Laughing she went down the bank, around the house to the street. "Ta-ta," she called. I stood looking at the grass.

"What did she say?" Miss Shelley called in her cracking voice.

"I don't know," I said miserably, "I don't know. I couldn't hear her."

The sun beat down between us and now that we were alone everything the woman was seemed painfully to flow into me, into all the parts of me where nothing had as yet happened and I was no longer myself but the woman I might become and the tortured woman standing in the door not three feet away kept threading through me like a taut wire that hummed and moved in my flesh.

"You must take some fudge," I heard her say. And that afternoon the earth, the sun, the summer air seemed to have in it something that was not for human beings in that Town, as if it did not fall on them so they stayed green and forbidding with never a good taste of ripe fruit. I wanted to start running and never come back but I thought of the endless prairies and knew that I would only come to another Town exactly like this one.

"You must take some fudge," she called out from the kitchen and I heard her cracking voice cold and drear,

"In the sweet by and by
We shall meet on that beautiful shore . . . ."

I didn't run, and in that moment I cracked the meaning in my teeth and the bitterness of it lay in me then, and I had to say it. In that moment I faced *it*, what had been coiling around the thought of Miss Shelley, what had been approaching, almost seen then gone; what had stood behind all the facts, everything men had been saying and women had been saying, so that what had happened became large, vent for their poisons. Now it all came from behind what had stood before it and I had to let my lips come over it and know it forever with what I would be able to find out about other things.

She had had a hunger just like me and that day they talk about when she was going and going after Hawk and they saw her riding towards the orchard in her new dress under her little umbrella, then she couldn't do it. She couldn't do it. She couldn't know. She couldn't risk. She wasn't able, that's what, she wasn't able. What nobody was knowing, what was standing in that Town over Miss Shelley's house was that nothing happened. Nothing happened! Except the wound that she gave to herself, taking a shot at her own breast. And the Town's rancor standing equally in them all was that nothing happened in any of them, neither sun, moon, husband, or child broke them open to good growing.

And I remember that standing in the sun I began to cry as if for my own lost life that had not yet begun and yet stood finished before me.

"Take some fudge," cried Miss Shelley peering from the door. "Take some fudge to your mother."

Autumnal Village

Why should he have to go out, now the summer is going, and shoot at the bright pheasants? I went as far as the spring with him this morning, and there were little cries of birds in the brush and our feet in the dead leaves, and I stood beside his lean body with the stooping head and the delicate pointed nose, and what has happened to me now that my love is a ghost, that the disaster of the Fall makes my blood fall in bitter cascade?

He looked at me coldly, with the leaves dropping around us. Are you sure you don't want to go? he said. I looked away to the hills and the village, now half exposed from their summer lushness so you could see the white spires of the churches and the brightly colored earth. No, I said, and saw the children running out of the house, calling down the hill.

He leaned over a little and I started back from the thin peck of his kiss. He stood a moment with his thin jowls close to me and I stood still so he would not find me out. Then he went down the hill with the Winchester through his arm and did not look back.

For a moment I felt like crying out and I stood holding my arms across my breast and the children came running in the wind behind me, crying, Mama — Mama, and then the two girls came eddying round my skirts, their hands upreaching and their cries like a confusion of birds, flying off into the autumnal air, around my head.

But when he was out of sight I forgot about him and walked up the hill to the great house he had built, not for me, but for his position, for the looks of it in the world, for the bargains he would be making because of it. O, it was a buckle to wear on his belt — the house, the children, and myself in fine clothes — a feather in his cap and bitter gall in my own mouth.

What could be happening between one moment and the next to change the heart in a woman? Here we are, it is Fall, and the leaves falling, the bare trees and the warm, still golden and green hills, the russet oaks and the terribly blue sky, the frail golden-light sliver of the tan grasses, slanting down the stems the way it does in the fall. The summer nests are now visible, hanging like pouches from

the branches. Everything seems close — the trees are closer
to the house — the road is closer and the hills move up.
The train in the valley is nearer. Next summer is white
upon the bough already. In death everything opens a little
to reveal itself. There is the heavy smell of smoke and
apples and wine.

Such a small thing to turn the tide of the blood
completely. If my brother hadn't taken the car perhaps it
would never have happened at all. It is nice to walk but
you never do it if you have a car, you only do it when there
is no car, and then you like it. Before this I couldn't sit
down in any peace, take a walk, give the children a bath or
enjoy the thick smooth surface of the world.

After he left we could see him walking down the hills
to the ferry and afterwards hear the soft ping of his rifle on
the hills that were his private preserve — where the signs
read over the forest — *PRIVATE. No Trespassing.*

Now, after the bright day, the night is alive with
sound. He has not come back from hunting. If he comes I
feel I will have to hide in the darkness away from him.

After he left, the morning was like newly washed linen
with little birds painted on it, and we walked to the village,
Marya and Ruth running ahead to pick berries. The village
is about a mile, and it was a pleasure to be walking in the
thin bright stream of cold fall air that made your cheeks
cold and fine, like the cheeks of an apple. Marya and Ruth
ran ahead and then back again, as if the bright thread of
autumnal space tethered them to me, giving them only a
space to run and pulling them back again to touch me with
their bright faces lifted, the blood mounting and falling in
their fat cheeks.

Marya would walk straight and single, her black bob
swinging like a bell around the tiny clapper of her face, and
Ruth a little stouter and more solid on the earth, setting her
fat legs straight down, her round face like some ripe fruit
hanging in the air; and crying out, they both were, with the
pleasure of it all, and how it was better than the city, with
frogs looking out from the brush, birds above you in the
sky and snakes quick into the goldenrod as you walk.

Farm women were gathering fagots against the winter.
They are sad but strong, walking and stooping slowly.
They have nothing to can this year. Women stand at their
doors. The tomatoes are no good so there is no piccalilli. I
feel young and yet heavy. It is bad to feel the sadness and
disgrace of one's own body, bloated with grief.

We turned the corner by the cedar, walking away from the river that looked as if it would flow on forever, full and bright. There lay the village with its tiny white houses and church spires like an old Flemish painting, amid the bare strong trees; and there in the doorway of the Rankins' house sat Mrs. Rankin offering her rosy nipple to the stout baby and Mr. Rankin standing beside her holding out a dish of apples. Their faces lifted to see who would be passing and the children slowed down, turning their heads to see the great mounds of the woman offering her white globe of breast to the eager child. We nod silently to each other without speaking and we can feel their candid gaze against our backs, and we are hurried along as if pushed with unwelcome.

Marya and Ruth wait at the post office standing back from the old odor of two ancient men who like crickets are leaning on their crooked legs, chirping in the doorway. I thought you were dead and buried long ago, said one to the other, and he answered in a high voice, I'll be around a long time after you're gone and measured all your length upon the sod.

The other said, You'll have to go a long way in time to beat me pardner. I aim to live a mighty long time from now. And they bent to each other, all their labors marked upon the turn of bone and the rot of flesh, like some half gay emissaries of death.

They looked from rheumy eyes at the passing of the children as they drew in like colts close to my flanks; feeling the hostile eye and turned shoulder of the village. We asked for the mail and there was none, and edged out past the two old men with the mark of their work like a signature upon their skin; and I felt ashamed of my heavy flesh and the useless weight of my grief, now heavy as autumn on my bones.

We went softly down the dirt road and we seemed to be listening to all the sounds of cry-to-horse and oath-at-labor, and the sawing of the winter wood in the forest before the men came home to lunch. We drew together, excluded from the common labors, conscious of their silent stare upon our backs. Why are we intruders now who own it all, the mills, the land, the seed. I felt like curious apology. . . . *If I am walking with my children, listening to the mouthings of ancient men, what is it to you? If I am walking, a woman, proud, unhusbanded, my flesh badly harvested as your land, in fresh wound and new*

*lesion, do you look upon me in grief too? I am walking on
this pillaged land too, and bear the brunt of those hunters
who have ravaged it. I am walking over this bridge, with
the thighs of the hills alive and the milk from the breast of
the wind, and a yearning with you to be alive and a long
way from measuring my height upon the sod.*

The soft sharp ping of the shots from the hunters falls
metallic against the hills, ricochets back and is killed by the
wind.

I feel again the dire and black shame of his lean kiss as
he hung like a knife above me, with the Winchester on his
arm.

The sharp ping of the shot comes from the hills.

We walked too far in the strong earth-day. Our
basket was full and the children full of the cold tang and
sleep. The echoes of the shots kept breaking across the
river, against the hills and then around the naked bowl,
from the waters and the earth.

We sat on a giant tree body, split down the center.
Half of it was standing. We looked up at the white meat
exposed and hardened. I said, the other half of it will fall.
Marya said, is it old as Father? I said, it is much older.
She looked at it, into the white bark split by lightning on
some dark night. It will fall, she said.

We were just walking, not taking any heed, going
under fences. Sometimes the shots of the hunters seemed
so close I was afraid we might be shot. But children in
bright dresses from the village went in droves through the
bare trunked trees and the cows began to go slowly in to be
milked and the sun went down steadily towards the south-
west slightly shrouded in smoke and haze. Marya and
Ruth walked ahead and the shadows of the earth moved
steadily eastward and we walked into them as into dark
water.

The children felt this, standing straight and no bigger
than little saplings on the edge of darkening shadow.
Look, Marya said, pointing to the down slope of a
meadow now darkening, the dark lathing down its side.
The bright dark, she said, and it did look so bright and at
the same time so dark. There was the strange death
glimmer of the Fall with this ghostly light. I lifted my head
to the pure frail light and saw Ruth and Marya standing, a
dark thin stroke in the light, pointing to the growing
shadow.

And suddenly, without warning, the sky looked like a bursting purple grape and the wind came out of a cloud like an explosion, and the trees looked like women trying to run with their hair flying, and the dark earth seemed to rear towards the sun and the black mane of earth rearing and running, with black foliage like blood from a horse's mouth and the full-to-bursting clouds. I felt a cry from my throat.

Someone shot from the lake. I took the children's hands and we started to run, falling down in the peaty bog. We climbed a fence and got to the road. We seemed defenseless. I felt I had never seen a road before like this, with only my two feet to take me down it. I couldn't recognize anything moving and tearing at its roots like this. We stood in the road and a little rain fell cold on us and then stopped, and we could hardly root ourselves in the road, the wind was so sudden-strong.

Before we knew it an old Ford stopped and two men were looking from their beards at us asking us to get in, and one got out and put out his hands and with one paw around their tiny ribs lifted Marya and Ruth to the back seat, and I found myself between the two men who smelled of oats and sweat.

Then the rain began to come down fast and the road to steam and the dry fields took it in. The two men looked out the steaming windows and lifted the old side curtains. Holy Christopher, they spoke in round and hearty words to celebrate the rain, and the smell from their caked clothes came out like sour buttermilk and the hands of the big man driving were like huge horned toads, and once we nearly turned around on the wet pavement and I could feel the children's eyes upon my back and knew they would be sitting still and straight, in homage to their own fright and to the terror of the world.

We went past farm and school grateful in the rain with faces pressed to windows, and women running to bring in the clothes, and sudden as it began it stopped and the sky looked like a wet bright stone. There was the rich glisten and turn of wet skin and feather. And the two men peered out with wonder at the passing storm, sticking out wet fingers to test the wind and speaking in a strange language of fallow field and rich, of rainfall, of winter, of the way it was so cold in March the lambing was no good, the seed barely came from the ground, and burnt were the rest entirely.

Will you ma'am, the driver said to me, the first words he had said to me, would you mind if we stopped in here at Ed Mason's for only a second, to find out if he has any feed he would be lending until our loans come in. Why no, I said, of course, and we drove up a bare slope of ground and stopped in the yard beside a bare frame house. A blonde woman and five children came to the door and a young farmer came around the barn. Some rain, they said, and nodded; and the men stood together talking and the woman and I looked at each other shyly and the children looked at the towheads and not a word was spoken but suddenly, like the rain, I felt happy and wanted to speak to the woman but I said nothing and the men walked back to the car paying no attention to us, lean as hounds upon their man problems. And I felt good for the moment and sat still and the men were laughing and the two big ones got into the car and still talked, saying that the Russian thistle was not such shakes for a cow, that it made her milk bad in a little while, with no butter, and that two years of drouth like this made the flesh bad in such a way that it was no good again to fatten it up, that the flesh was gone for good then and you had to breed it over if you wanted your herd A-1 again.

And the talk went on and I was sitting between the two farmers, feeling their strong thighs and the strong caked clothes and the great bearded faces so close to me with the powerful words like talons, and I felt full of wonder, looking at the lean farm woman standing there without introduction, and the children, and why was I outside the heart of this real happening? And then I knew that they knew the land my husband owned so they could walk it in the dark, and see a hill that they had seeded and stood in to the waist, and the women knowing the earth as close as a bed quilt to the hand. I felt my eyes open on a world I never knew. We got one lone mule, they said, to cultivate and the soil has been dry as a contribution box. Poor luck this year and that's a fact. Dry weather in the farrowing season, cold weather during lambing, and then they shipped the grass-fat weathers from Texas, putting down the price of our meat. It's a crying shame, they said, and the feed is higher and the prices lower, they said, and the corn is poor and seed is none too plentiful in the feed belt and the number of cattle on feed is pretty small. It's a poor year. It's a bad year. Well we gotta be going, we got to be on our way . . .

And the engine started, the woman raised her hand simply and I sat there dumb, the children waved and at the sound of the motor the red hens ran toward the barn like old women with their skirts lifted.

Where do you live they said, and I didn't want them to know I was *his* wife because they talked so bitterly about the mill being shut, so I said I'd get out at the bottom of the hill and they thought it peculiar but they let me out and one of them lifted the children out again and set them on the still-wet road. Thank you very much, I said, and I bowed to them. They took off their hats then and I was confused and felt the blood mount to my cheeks and I backed away and we half stumbled up the hill to the house. The rain fell off the great plumed trees heavy with their past living and their coming death. It fell on us and I took the children's hands and we started to run. *O you are wild young daughters* I cried to them, feeling my breast drive deep as the soil *O what wild young daughters!* And they began running and crying out shrilly and laughing . . .

There is the long hoot of the train. It sounds different on fall nights than it does in summer. In the summer it was like a festival coming through the green foliage, over the bright hills. Now it sounds like something sharp in the frosty night. The antlered trees are like black nerves jutting the thick earth. I can see the spring at the bottom of the hill where I left him this morning.

O what is the inordinate and terrible desire for physical life, the forest, the garden, the gentians the tiny bright hepaticas, the rain, hail, lightning, thunder, the wonderful flashing on the body of the earth, the day on the river, the children wonderful-solid, the bearded farmers, the wild dark-crusted earth like a grape.

You might get so filled up in the day with red hens running like old women with their skirts lifted, and two farmers with round quick eyes and a strong, strong brogue and the fog rising to fall upon us later in rain O he had a strong brogue to him, the one who drove, and what with the longing and the hunger in me he was like the sight of the hills and the fog rising and the wild turkeys walking strong and gentle up the saffron slope. O he had a strong male brogue to him, pointing out his precious bull standing with his cows looking out of the pearly fog, and his soft cows around him, so gentle, rolling a gentle round eye and loping gently with their swinging bags.

What puts such a fierceness in a man that when you see it you forget you've been without it? What puts such strong fierce marrow in a man that makes your breast ache inside your vaulted ribs to hear him barking out with laughter from his barrel chest that you couldn't be spanning with both arms. What gives him such strength in the day, such a brawny stance looking over the turkeys like a lord of creation himself?

The soft delicate little hills lying prone across the sky and the black dying trees like the beards on their chins, and them shaking their manes and their good eyes looking on the world of flesh and wheat and seed.

And running up the hill afterwards with Marya and Ruth, past the houses where farmers parted curtains to watch us pass, up the dark crest of rising mountain. We went running and crying out to each other, my children and I , and the hills were cold with coming winter and far ahead was the blue and lonely sky.

And the soft ping of hunters that I could not see, from the brush.

He is coming up the dark hill now. He will come in the front hall. He will lift up the limp bodies of the rabbits and show me how he caught them square between the eyes, and the bright bodies of male and female pheasants with shot in the breast and their necks hanging broken and their eyes half open in the voluptuous death he loves. He will be a knife leaning above me as he kisses me.

God Made Little Apples

"Yeah . . . yeah," Lars said. "Arrested . . . well, I'll be —"

"What is it?" the women clattered from the kitchen like geese.

Lord . . . so many women he had! He saw their fair fat flesh steaming in the morning kitchen, with the broth and coffee. "Well," he said, "what do you know? The old devil. That's the way for a man to act now after harvest."

"What is it?" Helga, his wife, said, turning her bright face. And the wizened face of his mother looked over the coffee pot, and there were the round laughing faces of his three big girls.

"It's Grandpa," Emily, the oldest, said. "Oh, Grandpa has spent his harvest money."

"Oh," Grandma said, "that old codger!"

"Yas," Lars said, swatting his huge thigh, "yas, the old man's in jail in Hastings — smack in jail and wants me to come get him out. There's a man for you. First harvest in four years and there goes the harvest money! Ho, ho, ha, ha!"

"Tch, tch, tch!" Grandma said, but she couldn't help smiling.

"Now, Helga, you'd have some complaining to do proper if I did that in the fall. It's a fair day for deviltry. Got a mind to go after him and stop and see Mrs. Potter I courted forty years ago, and would have married her, too."

"Gone on!" Helga said, flicking him with a towel.

"Tell us, Pa . . ."

"You're too young," he laughed, listening to the clucks, the warm talk of the women. He thought, "One good season can make a man feel good. Haven't been across the river for years. Wonder what Effie Potter looks like now; she used to be a sweet apple-faced gal for certain. Suppose I had married her." But he looked at Helga, warm as bread, opulent as his fields this year, mother of his seven children. No drouth in her.

And now the land, the weather, was with you again; the barn was full of hay.

"I'll go with you," Helga said. "The canning's done; I haven't had a vacation . . ."

He didn't know why he was set against her going. He wanted to get away from her, from them all.

"I'll get my things and go along," Grandma said. "I know how to handle these things. Every year at harvest . . ."

"No, you don't!" Lars said. "This is a man's affair. I think I'll join the old coot for a nip."

"Lars!" Helga said, and he saw her anxious eyes, blue as his mother's, and the great braids wound on her head, white now, as the snow of Sweden. "Mama," Helga said, "have you got the harvest money?"

"No," the old lady said, grinning in her empty gums, "he's the man of the family . . ."

"Twice a year," Helga said, "all his life, roaring drunk at seeding, at harvest!"

"You see what I tell you," Lars said, "you don't appreciate me."

"Lars," Helga said, "you're spoiled."

"How will we get him out?" the old lady said.

"I'll go get him out; I'll go this very morning. The cows are milked; the haying's done," And he thought, "I can go across the river. Why, I haven't driven over there in nearly forty years. I haven't seen Effie since her wedding day . . ."

He felt caught inside his life, inside the warm kitchen, in the golden hair of his women, his six girls. And he felt enormous, like a man who has been sweating at fighting in too small a space, a six-room house, ninety acres, where you plowed your sweat, and thought, riding all day on the sand, that it was like the fine hair of your Scandinavian women. Suddenly, he was greatly excited.

He rose in his chair, roaring for his good shirt, his Sunday shirt. "Iron it!" he cried, and stood in the kitchen roaring.

The women scampered like geese when he roared like that. He had on his clean shirt . . . Helga cut his hair around the edges . . . he pared his big nails.

"You're dressing up like your wedding day," Helga twitted.

"Might meet a brace of apple-cheeked gals," he laughed, and she made a face at him.

Then he got into the car, without a pig to market, without a bag of grain, free to cross the river into the fair, fall, country hills. Tiny villages, bearing the mark of men like himself who had come from his own country, seamen like his ancestors, with fierce scarred faces, tight curls and earrings.

He looked back and saw the girls waving, saw Helga by the door, and her kiss had meant, Do not get drunk. For a moment he wondered what is it — good year, bad years, your life, the sun shining down, women's faces laughing, a picture of your mother in a full skirt, mortgages making a ghost of the spoons you ate off? He waved, and turned the car down the road towards the river, through the village, across the bridge, up the river road and seemed to be driving into his childhood, his mother beside him, as she clucked to the horses and held him loose in her great skirts so he wouldn't fall. In the tiny mirror of the Ford he laughed, roared with laughter, seeing his thick pelt of a neck and one eye looking from the burned laps of skin pitted like the sand from his own hills; and the eye kept looking at him and made him laugh.

Memory lay like a thick mosaic all around him, a substance sweet and heavy. The wrecked and ruined houses, and the shapes of the strong men who had lived in them, thirty years before. There was the house of Strawberry Pratt, one of the first lumbermen. The house was empty now and the shutters flapping. The sawmills gone, the villages removed, a few white houses looking like New England, and some summer tourists. You passed cars with canoes on top and motorboats in trailers, and summer bedding and cookstoves piled in them. All along the river the old men stooped in the melon patches. And there was the store of old Sam. He could beat you out of your mother-in-law. By Heavens, he remembered the time Sam beat him out of a fighting cock, and he came away without the cock and with a couple of old hens not worth the powder to blow them up! Old Sam was dead now.

As he drove into the lift of the hills toward Effie's he thought he remembered certain trees, turns in the road, and a curious excitement made him drive faster. Her husband was dead now and she lived alone on the hill, her son gone away. He saw the barns empty. What harm was there in going to see Effie? Yet he looked down the road to see if anyone was behind him. An old collie came out to meet him after he had passed the windmill and the cream house, and a big rooster strutted past the wheels, and Lars laughed as if he had nothing to do but go traipsing around the country visiting old loves.

When he stood by the door looking into the cool, dark
summer kitchen, flavorsome, smelling of piccalilli, and —
did he imagine it? — the lavender perfume Effie used to
use, he grinned sheepishly to feel his heart hammering as
he waited for an answer to his knock. But he wasn't
prepared for the woman who strode from the darkness,
peering at him through the sunlight as if from the grave.
She was wearing an old hat and the face of Effie as he
remembered her hung like a dream in the layers of old
flesh.

"What do you want?" she said, peering blindly, and
the dead bird, hanging with dead claws to the hat, seemed
to see him more brightly.

"Howdy," Lars said, and knew that she didn't remember him nor ever would. She giggled and thrust the
hat on her rats, and he smelled beer on her breath. "I
thought maybe you had a calf to sell."

"No," she said, "the barn is empty. I tell you —"
She went on with the garrulousness of people who live
alone, as if continuing a conversation she had been having
many years in a lonely house with herself. 'I tell you I got
my troubles. Did my only son have a right to leave his
poor old mother?"

He stood awkwardly in the door, the sun shining on
his back, and the odorous dark out of which the old
woman loomed going over him like a litany of disaster,
over everything that she had lost, remembering every lost
thing, stove, chickens, child, husband, chair, cow, bird;
taken by flood, famine, cholera, graft, or natural decay
and rot. Her mind was like a huge and fabulous junkyard
filled with the idiocy of inanimate things to be lost,
maimed, forgotten, ruined, until he could stand it no
longer. But she didn't want him to go now, seeing his
hungry startled listening, and she followed him to the car,
clinging to its side, thrusting her ruined face at him.

And when he drove away, leaving her on the stone
threshold still counting up disasters, he felt sick and
wanted a drink, and drove away fast to Sam's tavern and
drank down two cool draughts of beer, before he felt good
again, and bought two hot melons which he thought he
would eat for lunch. The day was bright, lying under the
prismatic glass of sky, and the blue mist fell in the shadows
of the stacks and followed each fattening Thanksgiving
turkey, and he filled his pipe and began to laugh, thinking
of the old man in the cooler.

Afton was a village named by Scotsmen. It was a
nice neat village with cows grazing in the lowlands by the
river, an old hotel he had known as a child, little farms and
neat English houses. Many of these people had been
seamen like his own, had come at the same time, but he
didn't know them or they him. Only ten miles from his
house and he didn't know them from Adam. He had a
feeling for going in and asking them, "What do you know?
How do you find it?? What's up? How's tricks?" What
would you say? "Well, I've been living for sixty years ten
miles from you. Ain't it time we got acquainted?"

He stopped at the lunchroom and sat on a stool. An
old woman came down the steps from the kitchen. She
said in a queer voice, "What do you want?" and it
sounded as if it were coming from a throat caught in a
noose. He looked at her and saw where her whole throat
had been burned, shooting right up beneath her eyes. She
brought him some homemade cake and whipped cream,
and he ate, wondering how it would go with the beer. And
he still felt hungry, but he paid her, said good day, and
went out. The village street lay quiet, empty. He got into
the car and took to the road that went now into the hills, a
dirt road, lined with birches and grapevines and gold and
purple flowers of harvest blooming, goldenrod and gravel
root.

He drove along slowly, smoking, putting one foot up
on the door to cool it off; the lizzy got pretty warm on the
hills. He drove slowly because of the love he had for
looking at all the tiny farms on the hills, seeing the grains
all cut, the corncribs full, everything looking neat; but he
could see how they clung to the hills by the skin of their
teeth, too. He could read the farms like a book. It was
very interesting as he went along. He could see the signs of
struggle. "Bees . . . now they are trying bees," he thought;
"they think they'll make out with bees." Then someone
had tried raising peanuts. "You can't do that here," he
thought; "they'll find that out." And ducks and musk-
rats.

He knew how it was:

Always reading in some journal how if you got this or
that you'd be sitting in clover, all your troubles over,
everything hunky-dory. He'd done it himself, put in this
and that, pulled it out, found the soil or the climate no
good for it, that it was a racket. Ah, it was a fine thing to
look at the farms when they had half a chance, when there

was half a crop, and half a price. The animals looked
good, too, and he passed trucks full of squealing fat hogs
going to market, and saw the faces of heifers and steers
looking over the laths. He stopped once and some sheep
came to the fence and looked at him, and he looked at
them. He knew the hills would be full of berries and
grapes, but he felt too lazy to get them. He had done his
harvesting. He thought he would bring the girls down
some day and let them gather grapes and berries, but he
knew he never would.

He stopped at another tavern at the crossroads, where
an old man with a dog gave him beer, the dog walking at
the old man's heels. He drank down the beer and had
another. He didn't count the money spent. He was like a
man at a carnival who will cheerfully spend everything he
has. The old man sat down with him after the fifth beer
and had one himself, and they both lighted up and talked
about crops, the fishing, and the weather. And then they
got to telling stories.

They both laughed and their pipes went out, and they
lighted up again, and the old man brought two more beers
and told another story. They laughed and looked out the
window down the road where two carloads of fishermen
were just coming up from the river, their poles on top of
their cars. And the old man began to tell about when he
was young, and Lars listened and it seemed pretty
wonderful to him. And the old man got out some pictures
in an old cigar box that had a picture of a chorus girl of the
Nineties stuck on the lid; and he showed Lars pictures of
children now gone or dead, and of his wife, austere and
thin.

The old man said, "Why, sir, my wife was a saint.
When she had her first baby she didn't know what was
ailin' her till the fourth month. I was ashamed. I had to
up and tell her she was goin' to have a youngun. I felt like
a goat. She was a saint if ever there was one."

Lars laughed and said, "I got to be going up the river
and get my old man out of jail."

"I'd like to go with you," the bartender said. "I
know a man in Hastings who could fix it up. But there's
nobody to keep store. Should I shut up?"

"No," Lars said, "you shouldn't, what with hard
times. Nobody can tell how many pike fishers might be in
for beer between now and sundown, and want to fill up

and maybe want some hard liquor." Lars winked.

And the old man said, "I'd like a snort of hard liquor myself."

Lars said, "Sure, I would too. Why didn't you come out with it sooner?" He took a snort and bought a pint bottle for himself and put it in his pocket. Then he got into his car, the old man, like a broken stick, telling him where the turn was at the brick house.

"My own grandfather laid the bricks in that house and in all the viaducts around about, one of the best masons in the country. He laid every stone and brick worth layin' and was a boozer from way back, drank hard liquor like a baby drinks milk, and lived to a hearty old age, sound as a nut."

"Yes, sir," Lars said, and drove off toward Hastings, now only a few miles away. And he turned at the brick house and came to the corkscrew bridge which he hadn't seen since he was a young man and came here for his marriage license. That's why he knew where the courthouse was, which he entered and went down to the left wing.

The jailer opened the door, grinning, and brought the old man out grumbling. "Well, you took your time about it," in Swedish, and hooked his bones onto the side of the chair, folding his old bent legs under him, then said in broken English, "I told the old woman to send for you. You got to go to Thief River and get my harvest money out of the seaman's chest in the barn, and get me out."

"Why don't she do it?" Lars said.

"She don't know where it is," the old man said cunningly, "and I won't tell her. She might spend it."

Lars laughed. "I got other things to do myself," he said.

The old man said, "You get the money and get me out. It's a hundred and ten dollars."

"A hundred and ten dollars!" Lars whistled. "That's plenty. How much did you make on your wheat?"

"A hundred and twenty. I spent ten already."

"All your harvest money," Lars said.

The old man bent his head but looked from under his shaggy brows with one cunning eye. Lars had to laugh.

"Take a snifter," he said, offering his bottle of moon.

The old man threw back his turkey-gobbler throat, and it turned red slowly from the powerful drink. He took out a half pint from his own lean pocket and filled it from

Lars' bottle, quick as a wink. Lars began to laugh. There they were, sitting in the Hastings jail, as naked of worries as jays. By heavens, he hoped he lived as long as the old man, he hoped he lived forever.

Outside the barred windows he saw the tall black trees standing in the golden day. A fiery juice of life seemed to pour through his huge and powerful frame, and he felt as if he could bend the bars back and he and the old man could climb, like youngsters, through the window and tear across the courthouse lawn, escaping down to the river where they would build a raft and float down to Natchez in the moonlight.

He became excited as if he were going to do all that, and yet he knew that he wasn't going to move. He didn't want to move, sitting on the stool opposite the crafty old man who must still feel the wild burgeoning of the young liquor in his veins; must still feel it though he must be eighty-five if he was a day. Lars suddenly loved the old man. He put his arms around him.

"Don't take any wooden nickels. I'll get the money back. I'll see if I can talk to the sheriff." He wanted to appear young and important to the old man, as if he still had some power in the world because of his physical strength, his vitality.

"Good . . . good boy," the old codger said. "Good boy." And Lars resented it.

"I'll mail the money in tomorrow, I can't waste another day," Lars said at the open door as if he moved, enormously busy, in the processes of a swarming life already ghostly to the old man. But, looking back, he didn't want to leave the old man. There he stood, fragile as a cricket, his hands almost to his swollen knees, so little Lars could have picked up the strong stubborn bones and taken them with him.

The sheriff said, "But he does this every spring and fall. He's a menace — tearing down the highway."

"Did he ever kill anybody? You never heard of him having an accident, did you?"

"No," the sheriff said, taking a drink from Lars' bottle, "but that's because we always catch him in time. Danged if I ever see the beat of it."

They both grinned. "Aw, cripes," Lars said, "a man's got to have his fling; you know hot it is." They both grinned and sat a while. "Have another drink," Lars said.

"Don't care if I do. Well, it's a pretty stiff fine, all right, but them fly cops . . ."

"The old man's pretty canny when he's drunk; just as a grasshopper spitting juice, he's harmless. You and I are getting on a little, Sheriff."

"Speak for yourself, Lars; I'm as chipper as I was at fifty."

"Why, Sheriff, a man wouldn't take you for a day over fifty."

"And you, Lars Larson . . . it's amazing. They must take good care of you 'cross the river there. What keeps you so young?"

"Aw, you're full of taffy."

"Well, you get me fifty and I'll just have to have another snifter."

When Lars left he looked up at the barred window. Even if the old man was looking out he knew there would be no sign of it. He would simply look out at his son and the strong blood feeling would be tender between them, strong as the sweet day. He stood in the strong light feeling that tumult in his blood caused by seeing the old man, feeling his blood kin rousing him to this wild warmth. He stood under a tree and took a swig from his bottle.

He drove back swiftly; it was getting coolish. Once he stopped and tore the melons open with his hands and ate them, and they went good with the hot corn liquor burning in him. Driving through the hills, he passed the tavern of the old man and the dog, drove into the hills where the valleys were cool and dark and the hill tips rose, catching the sunlight. Letting the old car rattle down a hill he saw a marvelous orchardful of crab apples, and his mouth watered. By Jesus, he hadn't seen such a fine orchard of crab apples in many moons, the trees were loaded, they shone red and smart.

Without even thinking, now that the liquor was warm and strong in him, he turned in, drove up a turning road to a ramshackle house in the curve, and stopped the car. It was very still. Some ducks walked across to the water trough. It didn't seem as though anybody was home. He sat there in a little doze, guessing maybe he had drunk too much, and now his bones would ache, but he didn't feel any ache yet, only pleasantness. He could hear a bull kicking the sides of the barn, a steady thud. He dozed off, seeing everything through his half-closed eyelids. It all looked warm as if swimming in a golden syrup, and he heard a woman's voice from the house say:

"Do you want something?" He opened his eyes, and saw a woman in the door, her arm lifted so he could almost see the pit. She was shading her eyes, looking at him.

He moved his limbs; they felt heavy and fine. "Yes, ma'am," he said, feeling easy and hearty. He got out of the car. "That's a fine orchard of crab apples you got here," he said, going up to her, and she put down her arm and smiled easily.

"Yes," she said, "the best in these parts, if I do say it."

"Yes, sir," he said, "it's hard to get a crop like that what with pests and drouth, and tarnation in general."

She laughed, still standing in the door. He saw what fine arms she had, burned, and he could see the strong muscle turning on the bone, yet the flesh was ripe and full.

"How's chances for getting a peck of them apples?" he said, easy and slow, looking at her. She looked right back at him.

"All right," she said: "we ain't got any in the house, though. We ain't chucked 'em down yet. We'll have to go out and pick them up."

"Fine!" he said. "That suits me. I haven't been turned loose in such an orchard since I was knee-high to a grasshopper."

"Well, all right," her heavy slumberous voice said. "Wait and I'll get a basket."

He stood at the door rubbing his hands together. He felt heavy and fine. He wondered if she could tell he'd been drinking. Shucks, he hadn't been drinking much — just enough to put silk on his bones.

She came out with a bonnet on that hid her hair and face and made her body more noticeable. He walked beside her to the orchard and he could feel the strong easy swing of her legs, and her body settling down easy on each step, then rising and settling again. By God, he liked that — the way she walked. Her strong breasts hung down in her wrapper and she walked swiftly, stooping to pick up the apples in her brown talons. He picked up apples too, dropping them into the basket. On one side the apple was warm, on the ground side cool as a cucumber.

His mouth watered from touching them and he set his teeth into one, and the white crab juice sprang out on his mouth and chin, and ran into his fingers. It was a fine taste, and he looked at the woman while he was eating, and she went on swiftly scooping up the apples which she was

now putting into her apron and dropping into the basket
all at once. He felt like a slacker in the face of her swift
voluptuous industry, and he spit out the core and began to
pick again. He found himself picking close to her and he
felt heady. The orchard was silent around them, and as far
as he could tell, all the menfolks must be out in the fields or
gone to town with hogs or steers. Apples dropped from the
trees around them, or farther away in the orchard, and a
strange communication was between them as they walked
under the little gnarled apple trees of the orchard.

And he only half heard when she said, "I think there
was a wind last night. I think enough have shaken on the
ground."

He was walking powerfully beside her and he felt
again that strong and terrible desire. It was mixed with the
feeling of the whole day, some last redolence of the blood
before winter. He felt a fright to think of his towering
strength diminishing in him in ills, aches, and debility,
until one morning in some fall he would be old and dying
and could feel no more the plow, the hot resurgence of
spring and brandy, the potent flood of desire and life.

They passed through a grove of live oaks, and hanging
from the trees by their feet were two steers, freshly but-
chered, their entrails a-light in the sun, blood soaking into
the ground.

"Sure," he heard himself saying, "a right smart wind
down the valley." But all the time he felt the strong
shifting of her weight in a thrust of energy, and the
down-dropping relaxation of her whole body as she settled
on the earth, and he saw the long sweep of her hips as her
dress fell in front and slightly hitched in back.

She said, "My husband took the steers to market,"
and it startled him.

They were alone there then, and he felt the subtle and
curious surge of her strong bending hips, the rhythmic dip
toward the earth and then the slight rise as she dropped the
apples in her apron, which she held up with her other hand.
Then she lifted her head in the hot silence and he saw her
young and burned face from within the sunbonnet, and
most of all he saw her eyes looking at him as if he were a
young man in his prime, and her woman's mouth slightly
open and the moisture of her movement shining on her
face. And then she lowered her head again and filled the
basket.

He didn't move. It was very quiet with just the apples dropping. It was the moment. He knew that. The baskets were full, the sun was setting. He moved towards her and he felt her stiffen and wait. And he stood very close to her and as he reached for the basket he touched the golden down on her arms and he saw the turn of the young powerful flesh up the bone gleaming and sweating. His big brown hand tightened around the belly of her arm and she did not move. He felt her breath, odorous of apples, and the sun hot on one cheek.

Then he took the basket from her, and he knew the moment was over forever and he felt a kind of huge peace with the slanting sun. And he walked silently beside her, and it was as if she felt it too. He poured the two baskets of apples into the back seat and saw it was nearly full of the little apples, cheek by jowl. He ate another, fingering the round tiny cheek.

He turned to the woman, who stood by the well, her face half hidden and secret. He started to say, "How much?" But something in her forbade him, as she stood there, still accessible to him. And he knew he would always see her standing there in the long fingers of the sun, like the opulent earth, like the great harvest, like all of his life, open-handed, generous, sweet-smelling.

"I thank you," he said, taking off his hat and dropping it. "I surely do thank you." He felt his face reddening as he stooped to pick up his hat. And he still felt her generous silence as he started the car and called good-bye. And when he looked back at the turn of the road she was gone.

The dusk caught him before he crossed the bridge towards home. The village looked strange and neat to him, and he drove into his own yard with relief as if he had had a great adventure, gone through dangers. The lamp was lit in the kitchen and the girls' faces clustered in the door. He shouted at them, and went through, the warm hands touching him, and the bodies of the girls changing into women, and their bright tender faces towards him.

His wife stood at the stove. She turned her startled face towards him, not knowing what he felt, nettled by his absence. Supper was all ready and he washed his hands and sat down, and took a fresh piece of bread. They had baked that day, and he could see his wife at the stove looking askance, not knowing what had befallen him.

The girls at the table in the lamplight were full of questions, and he began to swing into his story, making it a fine one. He felt strange and looked at the faces around him, and they seemed almost comic. It was like some Swedish fairy tale where you leave a picnic, go around a mountain, meet a gnome, marry, live a whole life, and then come back and your mortal wife is just wiping up the dishes from the meal not half an hour ago.

His wife was frying potato pancakes; so she stood in the half dark at the stove, and he knew she was looking at him and hanging on every word he was speaking to them. Once he stopped and lifted his head. "Bet you don't believe that, Mama, eh?"

She snorted in the dark. "Bet you got drunk yourself," she said, "bet you had a girl with you."

The girls made little screams and clucks. He threw back his head and laughed and the girls laughed with him. "What do I need of a girl?" he said, looking around at the strong, gleaming daughters' flesh. "What do I need of any more girls?" And they smiled and were pleased.

He felt strong and fine. His wife sniffed at the stove, and he got up, pretending to get water, and he stopped on the dark side away from the lamp, beside her. And she kept on turning the pancakes cooking on top of the stove. The fire from the cracked iron flew over her face, and he could smell the good smell of her flesh and of her hands. He put his hand on her thigh where the children could not see, and put his wind-burned face into her warm neck.

She turned her head, laughing into her shoulder. "Lars," she said, "the children, please —" And her face was full of fright and desire and embarrassment. "Please, Lars . . ."

And from the darkness of his fields came the full rich lowing of cows.

To Hell with You, Mr. Blue!

He said, "It's much better to go on the bus. It will be over in no time." He and Ona were sitting in the bus station waiting for the bus to Madison, because it was better not to have any children now because — how could they follow the races then, and what about Florida in the winter?

"Dizzy Dean sure gave them a wallop," he said, turning the sports page.

"Yeah," she said, her hands tight around the new bag he bought her from cleaning up on the Cardinals.

"All right, Hon, here we are," he said, leaning down for her suitcase, his jowls lean over his strong teeth, his nervous hands still gripping the paper where it told about Dizzy Dean and how Ohio had just come through.

The bus pulled smooth and huge against the curb. "Boy, she's a beauty," he said; "look at that — streamlined — ain't that a beauty, Hon?"

"Yeah," she said.

"It will be over in no time," he said, patting her arm. "Goodbye, Hon. Send me a telegram from Madison, will you? Goodbye, baby."

"I suppose anyway it would look like you and be a ball player."

"Jesus," he said. "So long. I won't wait. I've got to see a fellow."

She saw him going lean and lone down the street, and hate gorged in her mouth like vomit.

She didn't know when the bus pulled out. For hours they kept plunging into the country and she lay back, sick. When I come back, she thought, I'll be divided. I'll be empty. It's smart to be empty. I'll be empty and wise. The mist lay over the dark plowed crevasse of the spring earth.

She felt him instantly, opened her eyes, saw him standing in the aisle, sharp and neat, changing his hat for a cap, folding up his flowered scarf like a woman, pulling his coattails apart to sit between them for neatness' sake. He was neat as a trigger. Her senses sharpened in alarm. A certain kind of moth comes out after night, with so powerful an odor, both repulsive and attractive, and actually seems to permeate your flesh, so if you raise your

arms or smell your own hands you would think the moth
had darkened your skin.

She looked through the glass at the swelling, chording
earth. She put her hands against the cold glass, against the
steel skeleton. She moved as far as she could against the
window away from him. They began going through a fog
that came in wisps at first in the groins of the hills and then
thickened like whey.

The bus kept going swiftly through Wisconsin. Wisconsin has a powerful beauty. The girls were chattering,
bold slender girls, excited by voyaging with strange men.
They seemed nervous and precocious, fabulously slender.
The man who sat beside her kept looking at the girls with a
little sneer around his mouth. He made her feel ponderous
and heavy. Women are not his gamble, she thought, oh,
no, he would hardly take a chance on that. Instantly she
knew he was a gambler. He seemed to be striking against
her making her feel as clear as a bell.

The big lanky boys started sparking the girls. They
seemed enormous, gay and dapper, but with such a physical emptiness they were like sounding brass to her. They
passed through towns, past the first national bank, library,
newspapers, picture show, and bon ton beauty parlors.

Finally he bent a little towards her, coughed into a silk
handkerchief, and said in a delicate high voice, "Look,
what time will we be in Madison?"

"I don't know, I'm sure," she said, coldly.

He looked with his down-slanting eyes at the back of
the seat in front, and she saw his nervous slender hands
with the thumbs turned back, hanging like delicate boughs
from his wrists, a little heavy. "My name is Blue," he said
to the back of the seat. "My family used to call it Bleu, but
now it is just plain Blue, that's what it is now."

She suddenly had to laugh, he looked so like a little
plucked cock. He had had sometimes a peculiar little
electric manhood in him, but now he looked exactly like a
little plucked cock.

"Blue," she said, pursing her lips to keep from a wild
snort of laughter.

"Just plain Blue," he said forlornly.

What had got him down so low? She said, "Are you
French?"

He looked at her suddenly in pure astonishment, and
the black hair going down his slim head seemed to stand on

end a little, exactly like a cockscomb. "Why, no one ever asked me that in America," he said. "No one ever thought anything about it," he said in utter astonishment, as if he had been going softly in the underbrush of America, hardly seen, laying his bets.

"You're a gambler," she said.

Now his cockscomb did bristle and rise right up on his tiny cranium. "How did you know?"

"Well," she said, "I thought you might be half Indian and half French."

"Oh, no." Now he was excited. "Oh, but no, *full* French."

"O.K.," she said, "full French. O.K. with me."

He leaned toward her. "How did you know I was a gambler?"

She lowered her eyes to his quick hands that turned over in the light like something turning out of the dark underroot, and the strong turned-back thumb and the whiteness as if they slept in the day and at night the tips knew the Jack, the Queen and the Ten. She couldn't look above his hands — she felt something dreadful would happen if she looked him square in the eye, she didn't know what. He turned toward her that soft curiously probing nervous energy. She knew he had huge dark eyes, very round and wide, wide open and dark and blank, his energy being in his nerves, in the nerves of the hand where you could see the thick gorged arteries that fattened on the lean backs.

"I am all French," he said, "I have crossed the ocean fourteen times, that is a lot, yes?"

"Oh, yes," she said, "a lot."

"Oh, it is wonderful, wonderful," he said in his peculiar alone little ecstasy. "Have you crossed the ocean?"

"Oh, certainly," she lied, "I have crossed the ocean." He would look down on her if she had not crossed the ocean.

"I went to Catholic school," he said sadly. Oh, he was sad, it came out of him like some dusk emitted from his pores. "My folks live here now."

They went plunging through the thicketed hills, now darkening in the dusk.

Suddenly he seemed to excite himself on his own whetstone. "Listen," he said, "I've had it easy, very very easy, very very very easy. I've had plenty of dough."

"Fine," she said.

"Oh, but it is sad now," he said quickly, ducking down, just collapsing beside her. "Listen," he said, "You wouldn't believe it. I could sit here and tell you about my life. I've been sitting very very pretty. I'm sitting very very pretty right now. Would you believe it?"

"Oh, yes," she said, turning her mouth down bitterly, "I would believe it."

"I don't know what it is," he said, "the bottom has dropped out of everything."

"Everything?" she mocked.

"Oh, everything. Look, here I am going around piddling around like this, making long jumps in the dark and what for?"

"I couldn't say," she said.

"To lay a bet on a horse. I have to monkey around like this because the law says you can't lay only so much in one spot. Piddling, a little dab at a time. Can you believe it?"

"Oh, I can believe it," she said, and she saw he had big circles around his great blank frightened eyes.

"Fighting, gambling, everything, what is it now?"

"Well, what is it? She thought she was going to vomit. She could wear him and she could wear her husband for a pin, or crush their tiny excited bones in her hands.

God damn men who are gamblers, baseball players, prize fighters, horse racers, driving a woman batty.

They whizzed through the villages at evening time. The houses began to be lighted, colts followed mares into the barns, children burned with the first sun were adrowse from heat. The bus stopped in little towns you could never see again. Two young girls came around the corner of a bank swishing and chattering. I was like them, Ona thought, now I am different. They were turning their mascaraed eyes towards trouble, trouble heavying on their bodies. I won't have to see it, she thought, I'll be gone. I don't have to see it, but you know it is coming like a cyclone. The bus leaves in five minutes.

They passed a woman driving two horses with tails magnificently braided and mud hanging from their winter furred bellies. She thought she would never forget that woman, as for an instant she looked into her wide hanging breast and at the child only half broken from her, still

moulded to her thighs. There she sat holding the reins of
the horses so they would not bolt, poised in the midst of
her strong life, in birth, crops, baking of bread. Mr. Blue
did not see her. He was silently sleeping, his head hanging
off his thin neck a little.

She had to look at him when he wasn't looking. At his
narrow shoulders, at his tiny pointed ears, and the black
hairs growing on his green white skin. She had to look at
him and she felt he was half awake like a cat. She felt
heavy and beautiful beside his quickness.

The sun had long gone. They changed drivers, this
time a stout strong fellow, very safe. The mist rose from
the river and began to cover the earth. Mr. Blue sat up and
looked into the milky dark. "Where are we?" he said.

"I don't know." She felt contempt for his little fright
and anxiety.

"Now, if it weren't for this law," he said sadly, "I
wouldn't have to be riding like this to Madison. I have to
go to Madison now to place another bet. Oh, it's
piddling."

"I have to go to Madison," she said, "I don't like it
either."

"Yes, gambling isn't what it used to be."

"No," she said, "it isn't."

"I've certainly had it easy in my time," he said,
spreading out his hands. "I've had plenty, plenty of what
it takes. Say, why don't you become a booker in Chicago?
Most of the bookers are women now. It's awful."

"I can imagine," she said.

"You can't go anywhere without stumbling over
women now. They get in your hair. Women are
everywhere, drinking, making the love, at the races. It
used to be you knew when a woman would turn up. Now
they're everywhere, throwing up along the curb, everywhere. Phew!"

"Yes," she said, seeing his huge distaste. She felt a
huge laughter in her. I hope they overrun your nice neat
little gambling world. I hope they spoil everything.

"Women are fixed, too," Mr. Blue said.

"Fixed?" Her blood ran cold. "Fixed?"

"Sure. They just want it and what they can get.
They're all fixed."

"So, women are fixed."

"Oh, but certainly."

"They're all fixed?"

"Everything is fixed," Mr. Blue said.

Oh, you could wear him on your wrist with a chiffon handkerchief, or like a lizard on your neckpiece.

The fog kept getting thicker. They only rose out of it on the hills where the moon rode the sky. Mr. Blue talked more in the dark. The lights were out and the driver had to go very slowly. They would · be in Madison at twelve according to schedule, but they were running behind. They would be late. She put her hand under her coat lightly. I hope we never get there. I hope we never get anywhere.

"So you're awfully smart, Mr. Blue," she said bitterly.

"Oh, I know the world from A to Z."

From a tomb, you mean."

"Oh, not bad, but I know it. I've been around. Oh, I've cracked that oyster O.K."

She had to look at his slender cocky head, the pale neck where the hair had been clipped, the odor of Sen-Sen and eau de cologne, the narrow faun's shoulders, the curious nervous body. Like her husband's. On the trigger excitement. You could crack his little head like a fine nut between your hands.

"I've been around. I've seen things, lady. I've seen 'em come and go. I've been in some pretty important places."

"Have you, really?"

"Oh, certainly. I'm not a ham. I'm going around now on this piddling business, but I'm no ham. I been in the big time. Don't you believe it?"

"Oh, sure, certainly, I believe anything you say."

"Fine. Well, it's the truth, I wouldn't fool you. Why, I was press agent once for Dempsey. The great Dempsey — you know, the great great boxer."

"Oh, sure, certainly, I know. So you knew Dempsey."

"Did I know him! We were just like that. Oh, a king, a prince, a man among men. I was with him. I came right out of the ring with him after that pretty knockout. Oh, that was sweet, the sweetest thing I ever saw. Oh, that night I'll never forget. That was the greatest night of my life. Oh, that was sweet, as sweet a one as I've ever seen. It's worth living to see that come over, swift and sweet."

He wasn't describing love. "Did you know his wife?" she said.

"Sure, of course, natural. I knew his wife."

"What's the matter? You look like you tasted something bad."

"It's bad for a great champ like that to get himself hooked up. A bird like that should never get himself married, that's what I say."

"That's what you say."

"Sure, I say it and I mean it. A bird like that shouldn't do it. It's a crime."

"Sure," she said, "a crime."

"Sure, a crime. What business is it of a fellow like that hooking up? Oh, that night I'll never forget it. Why should he get spliced after a thing like that?"

"I don't know, I'm sure," she said. She felt pretty bitter against him. "She's a nice person," she said feebly.

"Oh, sure, she's all right, but he's got no business. Why, a fellow like that is sitting on top of the world. He can have everything. I was with them after that and he could have everything. But prize fighting is different now."

"Is it fixed, too?"

"Oh sure, is it? Is it ever fixed! Look, wrestling is fixed, too."

"Is it possible? Women, now wrestling."

"Wrestling worst of all."

"Is it possible? You've cracked that nut, too?"

"Sure," he said, "I know that game, too." He grinned. "From A to B, too. Look, wrestling is fixed, stands to reason. Want me to tell it?"

"Sure," she said, "I'll keep it a secret."

"Now look, you could break a fellow's foot, couldn't you? It stands to reason. If it weren't fixed, why don't they break each other's bones? You never hear of it, do you? Why don't they if it ain't fixed?"

"I like to see it," she said, "better than hitting."

"Oh, sure," he said, "a woman's soft like that. But it's fixed. There's nothing as good as boxing. Oh, man, the sweet fights I've seen. But boxing is fixed, too. I don't hardly never go to a match any more. Minneapolis is nuts about boxing. I never go, though, since Dempsey is out of the ring. Boxing ain't the same since he's gone. The Champ . . ." He turned his blind ecstatic face towards her. "The greatest living champ . . . he was the greatest that ever lived . . ."

Love, O manlove in his voice. "So boxing is fixed, too," she said.

"Sure, boxing is fixed, too."

"I hope it's all fixed, Mr. Blue," she said.

The bus driver got pretty nervous. The mist rose heavy now and the encircled moon rode high amidst the thick thrusts of spectral trees and the fog flowed past the windows like milk. Suddenly they would rise directly out of it into a terrifying clarity that made them feel the cliff was striking them, that the moon moved into their faces.

Everybody got kind of nervous. The girls were half asleep lying against the shoulders of the young men. Mr. Blue got very nervous and wriggled in his seat, and tried to look out to see where the driver was going. The road was muddy, and they went very slowly; the driver had to open the door sometimes to get a line on the shoulder of the muddy road. When they struck an easy stretch Mr. Blue tried to sleep leaning forward, sharp as a needle, his head on his folded wrists; but she knew he would be half awake to see what would t happening, how the wheel would turn. He slept like a at ready to spring into a nervous spasm, or snarl in a delicate sneer.

It was really pitch dark out. You couldn't see a thing. The bus heaved them all forward and stopped. The driver wiped the sweat off his head and swore. "When we get to Madison," he said, "I'm going to jump in the air and click my heels together."

Sure enough, Mr. Blue sprang alive laughing. "I would like to see that, too," he said, chuckling soundlessly. An old man was standing bending his head against the roof, peering out. You couldn't see a thing. It was just like thick cream out. He was a serious grizzled old man bending over looking at the fog. He said, "Let me out." Mr. Blue said, "He's yellow. He wants to get out." Everybody heehawed. The half sleeping boys seemed to have gigantic faces with huge ear handles that they turned toward Mr. Blue. The driver opened the bus door letting the fog curl in like spilled milk. The old man stepped out and was whirled away as if he had never been. "Goodnight," he said on the wind and the driver mopped his head. "Good-night," he said to nobody.

"For Christ's sake," said Mr. Blue shuddering, "I didn't have to come on this bus. I can afford anything. I got money in my pockets and I come on this lousy bus."

Ona felt such a loathing for him. She could twist him in her hands until his eyes sprang out. "So everything is fixed," she said. The wheels spun in the mud. When the mist lifted it showed the soft dangerous shoulder, exposing their danger and frightening them.

"Look, why do I have to travel around in this lousy bus risking my life just to place a little measly bet?"

"What a tragedy," she said clinging to the seat, "a major tragedy."

"I'll say it is. Everything is fixed. Not what it used to be by a long shot."

Sad, oh sad.

He clung to the seat, his eyes popped out in terror, and he tried to peer from side to side into nothing. They struck a little stretch of half good road and breathed easier. "I used to enjoy," Mr. Blue said, his teeth chattering, "God Christ, I used to enjoy. Do you know I was with Wrigley's ball team? I used to go to Catalina and see them wind up every spring . . . I was keen for baseball, never missed a game, traveled clean across the country to see St. Louis play. And do you know I was right there in St. Louis the other day, had tickets for the game, and do you know?"

"What?" The bus shivered and threw them all over so she had to cling to the sill of the window.

"Oh, terrible," Mr. Blue chattered. "Why do we stand it? Can you believe it. I was right there on the spot and wanted to see Dizzy wallop 'em across and do you know I never went near the ball park? Can you believe it?"

"Impossible."

"Can you believe it?"

"I can believe it. I *must* believe it."

"I don't know what's got into me." The driver let the bus drop into a hole and spun the wheels and roared the engine and lifted heavily out. "I didn't have to come on this lousy bus and now look, we'll all be killed. I've got my pockets chuck full of dough and I buy a ticket on this bus."

She laughed silently and held to the window to keep from lurching against him. Come on, little man, don't get excited, take a little gamble on your white bones, shoot your own bones for a crap game once, darling, take a chance on your own dancing bones and you won't look so under a plank.

"Listen," Mr. Blue said, "do you think I am going to be sick? I'm getting seasick." He held his handkerchief to his mouth. "Listen, girlie, you come to Chi and get a job in the booking office, lay your money right and inside of a year you'll be rich, lay your money with the smart guy . . ."

"I don't care for it."

"What?"

"I don't like it."

"You'll make a lot of dough."

"I don't care for it. I don't want a lot of dough."

"Jesus, I do. I want a lot of money. I spend a lot of money. I need a lot of money. I can't stop needing it or spending it. I need it and I spend it. I don't have to ride in this lousy bus going through a fog like this."

The thick rich milk flowed around them. Miserably Mr. Blue rocked with the bus, his handkerchief to his mouth. "Jesus," he said, "so you don't want money. I can remember a long time ago when I felt like that. I wanted something . . . I felt that a long time ago. I can just remember it, imagine that, I can just remember . . ."

"I can imagine it."

"But, Christ, I need money now. I need things. See this suit? This is a hundred dollar suit . . ."

"Is it possible!"

"Yeah, feel that, that goods there, just put that between your fingers . . ."

"I wouldn't feel it for a million bucks." She wouldn't touch him with a ten foot pole. The bus heaved them all forward and the wheels spun as it hung in mid-air.

"For Christ's sake," said Mr. Blue, shivering in such utter sensibility and terror. The wheels spun, the engine roared, the bus groaned, pulled out and ground along the mud. "I can afford anything, can you believe it. I didn't have to come on this bus and I have come on it."

"I can believe it," Ona said. "Certainly, why make such a fuss? This is alright. You're a poor gambler, really. Do you just gamble with money? My husband, too. A diamond is an awful little spot to gamble your life on. What if Ohio did come through . . ."

"Don't get mad," he cried, cringing, lurching forward into his handkerchief and retching.

She felt like a roaring bulwark of flesh beside him, a tidal wave of woman's flesh, terrible in wrath.

"Why do we stand it?" cried Mr. Blue in misery, and he leaned his black fox terrier head on his white hands.

And she had to look at him as if his little black cranium bore her some secret, his tiny pointed ears, the

black hair growing like bracken out of his white rock
wrists. I know you, Mr. Blue. My husband, too. You
don't care for anything that doesn't touch you on the nerve
ends like horse racing, like seeing a horse you've bet on
come down the course, like seeing the cards lie right, like
seeing Dempsey move in with a neat haymaker. What
chance has a woman got with this? If the cards lie right,
what price a woman? — if the horse flesh comes in pretty
and neat, what's the use of a woman? You can feel that in
every bit of your delicate nervous twitching skin, Mr. Blue.
You can't depend upon ball players, card, dice, horse
players or prize fighters to make fat children drop down in
season. A soft luminous volume seemed to fill her body
like love for this earth.

In one hour they would be in Madison now. She
began to make a telegram letting the words form in front
of her. She felt large, delicious, wonderful and terrible.

She started and saw Mr. Blue looking at her with one
eye, like an animal in a thicket. Her blood shot and
cascaded down her in a terrible black fury as if splitting her
veins and thrumming against her skin.

"I was watching you," said Mr. Blue. "I'm afraid of
you."

"Yes," she said. She knew clearly the words of the
telegram. They came out of the fog, lifted into the hills
where little firs grew.

Mr. Blue's face drifted down sharp in the moonlight.
"What do you enjoy?" he said.

She couldn't cry out to him she enjoyed her husband,
gambling blood and bones then. She felt terrible and wonderful.

"Oh, I used to enjoy," said Mr. Blue, continually
wiping his mouth with his handkerchief. "God Christ, I
used to enjoy. Do you know what I enjoy now?"

"I couldn't say." The bus ran along now swift and
smooth.

"There is only one thing I enjoy now. Everything else
is fixed, could you believe it?"

"I could believe it. Shoot."

"I enjoy food."

"Food?"

"Food."

"Well," she burst out laughing, "for Christ's sake!"

"I walk blocks," he says, "blocks and blocks to get
something to eat, something very nice to eat."

"What, for instance?"

"Oh, something very, very nice."

"Like what?"

"Oh, I don't know, something nice, prepared nice, you know, tasty, seasoned up good. But this is hard to find. I have even gone to another town to get something better to eat."

"Is it possible?" she cried.

"And I gamble on it. I toss up a coin."

"With yourself?" she cried out, and the moon rode wildly through the pine. "With only yourself?"

"Yes," he said, "I make a bet with myself whether they will be having steak and mushrooms on Thursday night or on Sunday night. Sometime I gamble whether going to another town I can get maybe crepe suzettes . . ."

Oh, Mr. Blue, how desolate . . . how desolate.

"Madison," the bus driver said.

She pushed out of the bus. Mr. Blue cried, "Wait!"

She ran up the long steps to the telegraph station. She wrote as quick as she could: "To hell with you and Mr. Blue. I am going to have it."

We'll Make Your Bed

We were down in the hollow. It was a sunny morning and Slim and me were trying to be quiet so as not to wake Mr. and Mrs. Lamb who were on their honeymoon. We had the frame of the woodsy bed all set up by ten o'clock and Slim kept looking at the modern log cabin of the Lamb's and making remarks that had me bent over with laughing.

Slim was a fast one before the war and it didn't slow him up none, and he was making jokes about old Mr. Lamb the Lumber King taking unto hisself a blushing bride at the age of sixty. No getting around it, Mrs. Lamb was a looker, a nice soft woman. All the things you go through, I'll swan your old lady gets to be like just something around; you like her, she's comfortable as an old shoe when she ain't snapping at you like a bullwhip, but you don't feel it like you did at first and that's a fact.

"I hope mama doesn't come down here with our lunch. I told her we was raising old pines from the river bottom at ninety an hour."

"O Lord," Slim said, "don't worry, she'll be comin' round the mountain whistle time. No woman'd miss lookin' up at the windows of honeymooners even if they's old enough for a wooden kimono. She'll be steamin' down the hill and that's for certain and sure."

My old woman let out one of her tall whoops when I told her the truth at first that Slim and me got a job making all these little doodads for Mrs. Lamb, bird houses like little log cabins, cute as all get out, but as Slim said, "A hell of a piddlin' for two lumberjacks who in their day could blast a river and break up a log jam single-handed." It was bad enough when we had to fix up the old outhouse which was of good mahogany and Mrs. Lamb wanted it oiled up swank and a moon and crescent carved on it, so she and friends on Sunday afternoon took pictures of the thing as if it was a huge joke or something. It beats all when you think my old woman has been after me day and night to get indoor plumbing so the girls could be raised like ladies.

We made a summer house over the river and that was when Mr. Lamb said, "Boys, Mrs. Lamb wants a woodsy bed now." I couldn't stand to tell the old lady and I made

up the story about the deadheads. I couldn't stand the gaff
at home any longer. My old lady barring none has got
probably the longest, loudest, rip-snorting, rib-cracking
sneer that they is anywhere on this green earth. It was bad
enough when I told them about the woodsy bird houses
and the flower bower. My old lady is lean as a whip snake
and even if she has had eight kids on our old farm, four
dead and four living, she's fast and quick and full of
vinegar all right.

"Itty bitty bird houses," yell the kids like a bunch of
coyotes. "The champion, the birling champion, the fastest
man to twirl a cant-hook, works up to making itsy bitsy
beds for Honey" — this being what Mr. Lamb calls his
new bride. "Honey," says my wife, and the tone of it
would make a hole in a pine log, "Honey," she says, "Oh!
I want to bake my bread outdoors in an oven — oh, it is so
picturesque — it is so woodsy —" And Elmer, the spitting
image of his ma, begins to priss around saying in the high
voice of Mrs. Lamb, "Oh, make me a little woodsy house
hanging over the river. Mr. Lamb being an old lumber
maggot and all. . . ." And the other kids, like magpies getting in line, begin to jibber — "Lumber maggot . . . lumber
maggot."

"Good for you," says my old lady, bitter as lye. "So
after workin' your heart out forty years or maybe more in
these woods, you work up to hunting little saplings for a
woman that never bore a chick nor child. . . ."

I looked into my stew ashamed. "Well," I says, "this
is hard times — hard to get work — a man ought to be
glad. . . ."

"Glad," she explodes like stump dynamite, "glad!"
And I don't want to look at her for a fact. I went out by
the river and thought of the fine masts, growing straight
into the sky, I helped in my time snake down to the river,
down to the sea. The finest spars and masts that ever went
to sea we tooken right out of here. It was a fine country
then, with horse racing every Saturday at Stillwater.

"I ain't never stayed in bed this long in the morning,
even the first night me and Anna was married," Slim said,
looking at the honeymooners' windows.

"I guess a honeymoon is a honeymoon no matter
what age you're at."

We had set our sawhorses up far enough away from
the window so as not to disturb them none. We had got

pretty beech saplings from the woods. Slim and me, I guess, know every kind of wood there is being and growing in these woods. I remember some trees like they was people.

"When they get up," I said, "they're comin' out here and give us some good advice."

"The bastards," Slim said, "they better not come out here tellin' *me* anything about what to do with wood. They better not tell me how to make a bed."

"A woodsy bed," I said and he said with a snort, "Yeah, a blankety-blank woodsy bed." Slim has got quite a store of honeymoon jokes of one shade and another and him telling them all morning, while we was cutting the saplings for the posts, kind of got my dander up.

Then I saw her, dangerous and fiery like a flag on a battleship, coming down the hill with our lunch, tough and wiry, my old woman.

"Jiggers," Slim said, "there's the battle cry. Too late. . . . Prepare to meet thy God."

We pretended to be mighty busy and she bore down on us like a river full of logs let loose by thaw. I never was more scared. She just said, "Well!" and stood there like a little snake looking dangerous out of the brush. "Well," she said again and I had rather a fine bullwhip had curled lovingly around my middle. Slim was grinning, kind of sick-like, and pretending to measure the saplings carefully. "What now?"

I heard my voice break like a young fellow's and I thought the blood would burst my ears. "A bed," I said, hearing my voice squeak. She seemed to jump toward me. "A bed," she hissed.

"A woodsy bed," Slim said, and began to imitate Mr. Lamb, stroking a belly Slim didn't have since he got back from the war. "Honey wants a bed. She's got a dozen beds, some with silk, some with satin, but she's romantic so to speak — yes, Honey is romantic and she says being as how I'm a big lumber man — oh a big lumber man —" and here Slim batted his eyes in an awful way, winking and looking mighty fast and frisky and giving more meaning to it than the words seemed to, "yes, a big lumber man and well Honey it looks like she wants a kind of woodsy bed. . . ."

This even knocked the wind out my old woman and I could see her mouth kind of start to form the words "a woodsy bed." Just then we heard a door slam and voices

talking and saw a flash of color and there was Mr. and
Mrs. Lamb looking in all the birds' nests to see if they had
any birds and it made a kind of tickling fire come in my
belly to see them. Mr. Lamb had his arm around her and
she was a good full figure of a woman, with something
floating around her more like a nightgown than anything
else. And before I knew what I was doing I clapped my old
woman into the outhouse, told her to be quiet and locked
the door from the outside. I was back helping Slim before
I started to think and I could see Slim winking at me and
we watched them out of the corner of our eyes as they came
down the hill from the house looking into all the bird
houses, Mrs. Lamb kind of floating in this thingumabob
soft and clingy so I couldn't look at her straight. I thought
I could see the terrible eye of my old lady looking out the
outhouse moon Slim and I had carved.

I began to smell that whiff that comes from Mrs.
Lamb when she moves and makes you dizzy. My old lady
smells good too in a different way, kind of clean and soapy
and of babies. Not a bad smell when you come down to it.
But Mrs. Lamb smells like something else, I don't know
what, kind of indecent — and seeing them and knowing my
old woman is watching and Slim leering and winking at me
a kind of flame kept licking up inside me that had some
anger in it and something bitter as gall running sap deep,
strong and secret.

"They're lookin'," Slim says low, "to see if they've
caught any birds in their piddlin' little traps of houses. If I
was a bird, I'd fly over and you know what I'd do —"

"Shut up," I says. They are coming down to us
holding hands and old man Lamb kind of looking at her
with mooning eyes and she's laughing and swinging his
hand and stuff floating around her, all filled out a fine
figure, and like she never had worn herself to a frazzle like
my old lady. They are looking at the stuff that is coming
up and she kicks the earth with the toe of her shoe which
has a little fluff on it like the stuff around her neck. I
know my old lady has got her eye peeled to the crescent
moon and will be able to tell the kids all about it come
evening.

It's like when they come down to us that we are like
the birds or the stuff they have planted, or the woodsy bed,
as if they owned us like a dog or a cow, and watching them
I knew what my old lady felt. I felt it lick up my insides
like a snake tongue.

I got to keep a straight face because I am facing them all the time and it is terrible and comical to see Slim's big eyes turn over in his face as he winks at me and I see in his face too a kind of drawn look as if the fast, hot blood was pouring out of him somewhere. They are coming up slow now. Mr. Lamb says to us, "Hello, boys." A man used to managing has a way of speaking I suppose.

"How are you *Mr.* Lamb," Slim says eyeing down the board he has been planing and I try not to look at Mrs. Lamb because my wife will say I was looking at her all the time.

"Now," says Mr. Lamb, his pudgy hands over his paunch as if he has pride that his woman is a little foolish, "the little woman has changed her mind. She wants the color of the pagoda changed."

"What?" says Mrs. Lamb and I don't know if she is a little deaf or just doesn't listen. Mr. Lamb shouts out what he was telling us. "Oh, but yes," she says, "I don't want it yellow now. I will take all the color off."

"A hell of an idea," says Slim, keeping on with his work. "Should never paint a birch."

"What?" cries Mrs. Lamb, and everything she says she seems to jump and move in the stuff that floats around. "Nothing," Slim says and she begins to watch Slim's hands, tender as a woman's on anything that is made of wood. If Slim was blind as a bat he would still be a good carpenter. He can feel wood in his hands.

"The little woman has changed her mind," Mr. Lamb says, and I can hear my old lady telling the children about it at supper in his very words. "You know how it is with women."

We don't say nothing.

"What?" cries Mrs. Lamb again.

"About the yellow paint," Mr. Lamb says.

"Oh, yes," she says. "What will take it off? I could do it myself."

"Oh, you better let them do it," says Mr. Lamb.

"What about sandpaper?"

Slim spits a gob into the sawdust. "You can't sand-paper a birch. You'll have to get some lye."

"Lye," says Mrs. Lamb.

"Yes, lye," Slim says, taking a good straight look at her. "Something with bite to it."

She looks startled. "Something with bite to it," she says over again looking at Slim.

"Yes," he says impudent-like, I thought, so I got nervous and so did Mr. Lamb. "Yes, with bite in it. . . ."

Slim ignores Mr. Lamb. "Sandpaper won't do it," he says insolent-like, looking right at her as if he looked her up and down.

"Oh, no," says Mr. Lamb nervously, "something with bite to it. You boys get some lye, whatever is needed, at the store, charge it to me, get whatever is needed to fix up the little woman with what she wants."

"Yes, sir," Slim says and Mrs. Lamb seems excited and begins to run around pointing here and there and it must be I imagined it that I could see that black snapping eye looking right out the crescent moon of the outhouse.

"Now," cries Mrs. Lamb, "I just bought two hundred dollars worth of grills and things. I am going to make an outdoor kitchen. They have such wonderful things now for roughing it."

"Two hundred bucks!" I says. I ain't seen a hundred bucks at once since the lumber went out.

"I am going to get back to simple things." She turns and clasps her hands and her fine hair seems to have fallen a little out of a net. "Yes, back to the simple life. That's what we must have."

"The simple life," Slim snorts, and Mr. Lamb gets more nervous.

"Well, how is it going to look, boys? How is it coming?" Mr. Lamb seems forcing himself to be hearty and gay. Slim don't say nothing so I says feeling foolish-like with the eye of my old woman glued on me like a vise, "O.K.," I says, and feel foolish to hear my voice break again in a funny embarrassed way which makes me mad enough to pick up a sapling and lay around me like crazy.

Mrs. Lamb lets out little noises, touching the posts like a ring dove in mating time, fluttering around Slim, who keeps right on planing the board, the shavings falling around. Mr. Lamb says everything twice to Mrs. Lamb, who listens as if she is dreaming and then lets out a little cry as if she is astonished.

"Oh," she jumps and cries around us so you can feel what a fine figure of a woman she is, smiling at you with her painted ripe face. Even from where I am with all the smells of the morning and the fresh smell of the shavings, I can smell her. "Oh, you must have had a hard time finding these wonderful trees for the posts, all four just alike."

Slim doesn't peep so again I says foolishly, "Yes'm."

"They're just beautiful," she lows, "just beautiful." And she comes close to Slim, putting her hand on the saplings, and I can see the back of Slim's neck kind of swell and the back of his ears get red. He moves away, picks up a hammer and makes little nervous jabs like a woodpecker.

"Well," Mrs. Lamb laughs, "I don't understand how you are going to make it. Will you tell poor me about it? Squeezics says I'm the most helpless —"

"That's what she calls me," Mr. Lamb says nervously. I thought Slim was going to laugh right out but he kept on making little taps with his hammer as if everything was falling to pieces.

"Now will that be solid?" Mr. Lamb says, picking up one of the posts. Slim takes the wood away from him. "Solid as a tree," Slim says, and keeps tapping with his hammer. Mr. Lamb picks up another one and feels it with his hands and Slim takes the log away from him and puts it back on the saw buck. "Strong enough," Slim says, looking at Mr. Lamb. A slow, yellow color seems to come over Mr. Lamb's bald head and then it gets very white.

"It must be strong," Mrs. Lamb says, her eyes wide, looking at Slim.

"Those are A-1 birch saplings," Slim says, taking another one out of Mr. Lamb's paws. "They're strong as God made them and you don't want them any stronger than that."

"Well, it wants to be solid," comes back Mr. Lamb, and his mouth looks grim and he picks up the log from the saw buck.

"It will be all right for you," Slim says.

"I'll tell you how I want it," Mr. Lamb says and Slim takes the marked sapling out of his hand and this time Mr. Lamb doesn't pick it up again.

"I'll tell you how we're makin' it," Slim says. If you know Slim you know this is just before he gets mad and tosses everything out the window. It's a good thing they don't know Slim the way I do. Then he says, "We'll show you how it'll be." So him and me set the bed up. They can see what it will be like and he is holding one side and I am holding the other side, and I don't know what he is up to. His nose is kind of pinched and white. I know this is a bad sign.

There is the framework and we're holding it up and Mr. Lamb looks very wise and says, "Mmmmmm." Mrs.

Lamb looks like she ain't seeing anything but Slim and she moves closer to him. "Oh, yes," she says and I see her put her hand on Slim's arm and I see the line in his jaw drawn tight. He moves away from her, and brazen, she follows him standing close, and we all look at the damned bed. "And then" says Slim, biting his words off sharp, "we'll put her in the river and let her soak. . . ."

"Oh, will you do that?" Mrs. Lamb says, looking bold at Slim, and I feel ashamed. I just look down at my hands holding the bed and I feel ashamed, and ashamed my wife is watching from the outhouse.

"Now I understand it," Mr. Lamb says and Slim looks at him as if he didn't know how to button up his pants.

"How will you put it together?" Mrs. Lamb cries and there is something like the way she smells in her voice. "This is too, too wonderful. My friends will be crazy about it. You might get a lot of work." Her eyes are big and bold on Slim. "You might get a good deal of work because if this is a success, all my friends might want to have woodsy beds. Just think of it. . . ."

It was that did it. "I'm making no more woodsy beds," Slim says. He pulls away from her and the framework falls to the ground.

"How will you put it together so it won't show?" Mr. Lamb says very important-like as if he knows all about it.

"Screw it," Slim says.

"What?" cries Mrs. Lamb.

"Oh, yes," Slim says as big as life, the white line showing along his jaw, "we'll have to screw it."

Mr. Lamb comes to and shouts at Mrs. Lamb, "He says they will have to screw it."

"Oh, yes," Mrs. Lamb says kind of lazy, her eyes bigger than ever.

"It won't hurt the wood none," Slim says, "won't hurt a thing."

"Oh, certainly," Mr. Lamb says too loudly.

I feel good for the first time, like a big spurt of laughter and strength came into my stomach.

"Oh, but yes," cries Mrs. Lamb. "How wonderful. I understand."

"Yes," Slim says and I know now he is going to do something for sure and certain. 'You better understand."

"Come in, Honey," Mr. Lamb says. "Breakfast I am sure is ready. All right boys, go ahead. Go right ahead.

Get whatever you want. Charge it to me. You know what to do. I'll leave it to you. Get whatever you want.''

Slim stood with his hands clenched big as tree bolls. Mr. and Mrs. Lamb went up to their house and Mrs. Lamb looked back. "The bitch," Slim said, loud. He picked up the framework of the bed and holding it above his head, with the heinie still from the Army, he walked to the edge of the bluff. Quick as a flicker my old woman darted out of the outhouse and she picked up the saplings and I saw her running after him, her body like a bat out of hell, for all the hate and sorrow of her life. And I felt this flick of strength up my neck and love for that strong tough flicker of a woman. I stood beside Slim laughing and throwing the last birch into the river. I am laughing so that Mr. and Mrs. Lamb turned at their house startled and frightened. "Charge it to me. Get whatever you want. You know what to do."

And my old woman began to laugh and she slammed me on the back and I saw her black whippersnapper eyes, looking at me again, in the same harness, the good bit in our mouth, together again. "Oh, an outdoor oven," she cried, flouncing like a witch, and Slim and I looked at her bitter strength like a fine aged wood. "Oh, a woodsy bed," she cried.

I haven't shouted across the river like that for a hell of a time. I opened my mouth and bellowed and it went down deep and came out strong, "We'll make your goddamned bed. . . ."

And it struck the rocks across and echoed back as if we had friends across the river — we'll make your bed — we'll make your bed.

Our laughter echoed back too, striking, emerging in air pockets, on wind currents until all the hills and old trees left rotting on the river bottom took it up, shook it out, beat it up and threw it back.

Song for My Time

It was a sad thing going to my sister's after we had the news of Bud's death. It was the first August without the big war and it seemed in many ways to be still going on. Papa had had a letter from his sister in Germany asking why she was alive when so many were gone. "I have a right to die," her letter said. Papa sat a long time with the letter without lighting the lamp and the cattle crying to be milked.

The train ran smooth through all the farms and villages and they looked the same. It was hard to think of hundreds who were gone and would not come back. When the train stopped at Horicon I got out of the glassed coffin into the sweet air, the earth hanging in blue harvest, the corn racing to ripen before frost, late this year, and only one round to go. And Bud would not be there for the harvest moon husking this year. He was the champion. Why did he have to go to Spain in the first place, far from Wisconsin, and now dead in this war? Papa was always asking this and I asked it now smelling the milky wheat chaff and the long bow of the hills let a sharp arrow to my breast, and I felt bitter as milk weed that my brother would not have the comfort of those little hills for sleep with our grandfathers, who gave us comfort too on winter nights, thinking of them beyond the copse, their fierce eyes closed, their stubborn beards thrust to the skies, lying in the earth we had cleared, cut, seeded and salted every year.

I thought for the first time then of death. Heavy with absence and remembrance I felt it rise in me from papa's sister's letter like the graved earth and death seemed inevitable and good. When you think of death there is a shift of focus and the light darkens a little. When I went back into the airless coffin of the train, I saw for the first time into the eye of the old woman across the aisle who had gotten on at Madison. She looked like a hollow reed, her face the anonymous one of sorrow, and with the bitter odor of weeds after frost.

I had an impulse not to sing my sorrow alone, a single song, my heart breaking now with the sorrow of not seeing him dead, with the final knowing of the body, and I wanted to put him with all brothers who are gone, not mine

alone. But I could not feel it. I could not say that any grief
was equal to mine, nor any absence more than mine.

I sat beside her and she continued speaking, her voice
light and hollow, single and alone. She did not look at me.
"I blame them," she said, "I surely blame them. I got as
far as Madison and there was a wire saying he was dead, no
use to come. I blame them. They used him poorly. He
thought it was his duty. A hundred and eight missions.
With a hundred only he might have lived. Do you think he
might have lived?"

"At least," I said, "You can bring him back to home,
but me . . . "

But she did not hear me. "I blame them, I surely
blame them. . . ." I was angered so I thought if I did not
move I might strike the closed face, the still lipped mouth,
the thin energy of age which seemed to feed gluttonously
on grief. She did not mind when I moved away but lipped
her grief in little morsels.

When I saw my sister coming towards me I wanted to
get back into the train, go on, because the cut of the bone
of her cheek was like Bud's and her hand held out to me
was the hand of my brother and I drew back seeing it
suddenly cut off, the strong flesh of milking and husking
muscles gone from the bone. I pulled away from her
embrace and the sight of her son, growing tall too with the
same family jaw and the blue eyes like Bud's and I resented
his shining face, the green sap life in his bones.

I thought I could not stay in her warm home. They
seemed to have forgotten. They were boiling kettles of potatoes and eggs all evening to make potato salad, for which
we are famous, to take to the Union picnic. "But that's
Bud's Union," I said, "The one he worked so hard to help
make, when he came back from Spain."

"And boy," my sister's son said, "Would Bud like to
see it. It's grown. It's wonderful."

"I don't see how you can do it," I said, "Not even
knowing where he is buried." And happily I saw her face
darken as if water three feet deep poured over it.

"He would want us to go," the boy said.

"A lot you know of grief and sorrow," I said, "Or
what it takes to make a man, a young whippersnapper like
you." I saw a thing rear in his neck, spring into his head,
make a hollow of his mouth from which no words came
and he turned, bumped into the door, found it, and went
out.

My sister looked into the kettle of potatoes. "Four from his graduating class died at Iwo Jima." And for a moment I felt the stone of my grief crack asunder. But it was solid round my heart again when she said, "You know who will be there Mona, Bud's friend Steve from the Lincoln Brigade . . . "

"I can't . . . I can't . . ." I said and the black grief ran inside me like an underground spring I saw once falling over the mossy face of a white rock.

But it was on account of my sister's son and the way he stood in the dark of the stairwell that night shyly asking me to go. I felt him young as I knew my brother once, when the sweet blood jetted in us in unutterable swiftness and pleasure with not a shadow of the violence that was to come.

I told them I would sit at the table in the grove with the lunch and they could go have a good time at the concessions where already people gathered around, the band playing and the cries of the barkers and the meeting of friends from far places. They left me there under a sycamore which was Bud's favorite tree and I had to turn away to keep from seeing his face in the shifting leaves and the spotted bark as he used to grin down from his house in our sycamore tree.

Then I began to watch the people. I could not understand it. They poured in a bright stream off the interurban. They came in old cars. They dropped their babies in the grass. A group of tall dark people of a kind I had never seen took the table next to ours. I could not take my eyes from them. One young man, his unaccustomed shirt white as snow, was making cracks in a foreign language about all the young girls. The eyes of the older women rolled knowingly over the heads of their suckling children. And fright struck in me like a bell. I could not understand how they could go on and on in all the risk and danger. They had been in the war too, nobody on the wide green earth could keep out of it all now. I could not understand how they laughed on a day in August, filled the earth's grass with their fat and merry children. The grief ran in me over the dark moss. I could feel it in my throat. I said my aunt's words, forming them secret and alone — I have a right to die.

"Are you Bud's sister?" The voice froze my face like stone. I nodded. "Well," the voice was strange as if it came from wood. He did not ask if he could sit down, but he did. I felt him beside me. "Who are those people at the next table?" I asked.

"They are comrades from Haiti, come to work in the beets," he said, and I had not heard that word "Comrade" since I had heard Bud say it. I turned to look at him and he took his corn cob pipe out of his teeth and smiled at me, as if bowing a little. I had never seen such a face. He was small, almost warped, his body wrenched, twisted but so strong I knew it was from the labor he had done. He was like a gnome, his head bashed in on one side, half his teeth missing. A long cut severed one cheek in a white ridge and you could see where it had been sewed up. And in this battered flesh his eyes hung big, the biggest eyes I have ever seen and they were sad, but they were also strangely merry.

A soldier came through the grass, carefully trying to ride the uneven ground with one leg and a crutch. I tried not to look at the empty trouser leg which hung almost from the hip, but I could not help seeing how the stump moved forward out of memory for walking. The gnome said to me, "Today would make Bud happy. All these people . . ."

"I do not want to talk about my brother," I said, and waited for him to oppose me. But I could only smell the strong odor of his tobacco and I found myself wishing he would tell me about Bud and the Union, for we never knew much, only Bud's letters saying he was working hard in Milwaukee and then his coming home thin as a rail and half sick and we just got him fattened up when there was Pearl Harbor.

I found myself waiting for the little gnome to speak. Out of a pouf of smoke he said, "I always figured the finest thinkers come from plowers. Bud always figured out why he did things, why things were like they are — a thinker."

I never thought of my brother as a thinker. After awhile he spoke again. I seemed to be overhearing him. "It's different today than the first days when we stayed up all night and ran off leaflets and got to the gates at dawn for the first shift and they would throw them away like as if they was poison ivy. It's different today . . ."

"Different," I cried bitterly.

He seemed to move closer, "Yes," he said, "Now with mining you have no time to think, or on a power machine or in a saw mill. They are raffling off a quilt. We'll walk over, lots of your friends are asking for you."

"My friends," I said, but before I knew it we were walking towards the hub of the activity and he had his hand lightly on my elbow. He came hardly to my shoulders but he seemed powerful and he talked to me all the way and I never heard such talk as if he knew every tree he had laid his ax to, even now when age and rheumatism had slowed his skill and power after he had built a hundred barns or more, drawing off the prairie wind, neat as water on a gentle slope. Now he had a bad job spraying furniture, but a strong man he said is like wood, a green sapling breaks, but not a man. "Now you take Bud," he said easily and it seemed better now to hear the name spoken in the afternoon. We stopped under a grove where a group of old men sat around a lamb and one of them turned the skewer over the hot coals. "Now Bud," he said. "Different things season a man. The labor movement made a strong man of Bud. . . . It takes heat and fire, the right temperature, the right cooling . . . the right winds on the right day, slow freezing. Bud was a man rightly tempered in struggle and the love of brothers."

I felt as if I had never known my brother then. I stood silently in amazement. His words were so strange, like nothing I had ever heard before. He spoke of a writer named Gorky, something about a story he might write about Bud. One of the old men around the lamb unbent his legs, stood, bent and spoke to the one who was turning the skewer who looked at me, his leathery face smiling. I stood embarrassed as the risen man came toward me. He was small and neat as an animal and he bent his dark fleecy head in a little bow and said something in another language. I looked at the two men so strange to me and the gnome smiled and nodded, his merry eyes containing us both. He turned to me. "He wants to tell you he knew your brother in Spain. He was with the Polish antifascists. . . ."

"In Spain," I cried. How could people know each other this way? I did not know them this way. I felt alone. They both nodded and smiled. "Yes . . . yes . . ." they both said eagerly as if holding something out for me to take which I could not even touch. The lamb turner cried out something and threw his head back and the others spoke sharply, a sudden excitement like a fire in a wind between them. I was startled. I looked from one to the other. I hung to the face of the old gnome. He took his pipe out, "They say those who struggle know each other. They say to tell you the fight against fascism is cheered everywhere."

I could not speak. I felt mutilated, more so than the soldier I had seen. I felt less human than these people and deeply ashamed as if they might secretly seize upon the contraband I carried, as if my thought of death might be written on my flesh as violence on the flesh of the soldier, as struggle upon theirs. I put out my hands and felt the fire. I smiled and tried to bow as they had done and as we passed on felt their warm glances, heard their strange excited speech, smelled the round roasting of the lamb. "We will have some when it is done," the old man said.

We passed into the tense circle of noise and pressing bodies. I looked now into each face to read its history there. Are they like myself, I thought, striking with fear and terror. I saw far off the people lying on the grass, and the children playing, summer and men and women marking their space upon the earth, close packed in the nut of the world.

Then I saw him. Bud had brought him to the farm once. He was sick then with his teeth falling out from Spain. I was afraid of him. It was Steve. But I could not get away. He was pushing through the crowd and he came up, his face shining with moisture, his eyes black as I remembered. And perhaps it was the strange sympathy of the heat beating upon us all like a tide going through us, but he spoke my name and put his arms around me like my brother, smoothing my hair. I stood there struggling not to cry. When I looked up, it was not Bud's face and he was smiling. I drew away.

"Come dance," he said and did not wait for me to answer but drew me away from the old man who was smiling in a cloud of his smoke. As we went into the pavilion I saw the women sitting along the sides fanning their children and they smiled at me and I knew they spoke softly to themselves, "Bud's sister." All around the dance floor they smiled. A couple poked Steve. "Hy Steve. Don't be a hog. . . ." Steve stood beside me. "Bud's sister." "Yeah," they said pressing my hand. "Yeah, we know."

Steve opened his arms and timidly and strangely I went to him. "I just got back from the Pacific myself," he said with that strange warm smile they all seemed to have.

"You too," I said, "Why did you both have to go?"

He stopped dancing and held me away. "Why?" he said. Then he drew me to him again.

"Yes," I said, "Spain. Everything. . . . Don't you get tired? My aunt in Germany is tired. Papa is tired. I —" I thought of my own death and I could not see the bready women and the pavilion.

"Tired?" And I was astonished to feel his whole body laughing and I looked up and saw him laughing. "Tired," he cried and it seemed to be like the speech of the old Greeks and Lithuanians around the lamb. "Fascism has a smell. You can smell it anywhere once you get to know it. It worries your snoot like a hound dog in hunting time with a wolf prowling the sheep. You want to be at them. You can smell it," he said again and I could see the wings of his nostrils flare baring his white teeth a little.

We went back but the lamb was not done yet. "In a little while," they said with hands, gestures, and we nodded and Steve said something in Spanish and they all saluted him with some shout and much laughter.

I heard a man's voice through the loud speaker. "The speaking begins," Steve said. We pushed into the packed crowd. They parted smiling, and some took off their hats when they saw me. I saw my sister smiling at me and her son came and proudly stood beside me. "How do you like it," he said, and I did not answer but I smiled. I stood on tiptoe to look over the many heads. By the pavilion three great horns blared out. A man was speaking introducing a woman from the Union who surprised me the fine way she spoke, then the soldier with the leg gone spoke very slowly, saying he could not speak but there was great silence in which his slow words fell, solemn and respected. One of the dark Haitians spoke very swiftly in his own language which some understood. Steve stood close beside me and explained things, bending down as if I were a child. I was caught up like those around me, listening, and suddenly it seemed I felt all their suffering with my own, it entered me like the heat and the closeness of their bodies, all under the vast sky, and the sun a golden hammer pounding, penetrating the web of man who stood alive, erect in his own courage.

Then they all stood without moving except on the edge when some baby cried or some boy ran in, thinking himself a guerrilla or one of the 34th Division in which so many of their brothers fought. The speaker was a man like many there, short, strong, a worker, and in his strong blunt hands he seemed to hold many threads that connected with all parts of the earth. There in the August day of Wisconsin we saw caves in Yenan where men and women unnamed, their place unmarked on any map, worked in dim light, day and night; and below the earth we saw small groups meeting in little rooms with serious faces. He named and spoke of all the countries, and the earth seemed to become whole as an apple and they were woven all together with the Wisconsin earth and history and the dusk was peopled. The woman on the edge of the platform gave her breast to the young one and the speaking went on as if smiling warriors came up from the dusk, and we were all warriors and the speaker mentioned us all, every one, as if every man on the earth had a space of dignity and stood in the light that included all others. I thought then how great was man when he was most human and I looked at Steve and knew how my brother loved him and he seemed so tall I knew there was something taller than we knew about the human man when he was most human just as he was most paltry and ridiculous when he was burlesqued and defamed and cruel.

I did not draw away when Steve took my hand. I stood there while they clapped as the speaker finished. I was running manifold over the earth the trees like birds running with me. I listened to the tide going and the sun a golden hammer. Then I heard my name called and a shock went through me. They were all clapping and pushing me forward and the old fright went through me and terror and aloneness. But they thrust me forward on their hands and I was standing on the platform, lifted there, and when I turned I knew the saying of my speech was something that I had to have courage to do, and with not my little fear to cripple me, so I began hearing my voice, strange and small, saying as I felt I had no right with death so near in my mind two hours before, that it was nothing I had done yet, only my brother who belonged to the body of my life and of the earth's. I saw them all there smiling that smile I had never seen before as if they loved me and I had to say further that we were all together and I saw the young girls in white dresses who had been walking restless all the afternoon, their arms entwined around fragrant waists, stop to listen. For the first time in my life I felt the draw and pull and strength of something outside my own mouse grief. I believe my voice strengthened. I had a feeling of great power as if it would grow and enter every being. I said, using the only language known to me of fertilization and growth, that this is a dark time, the seed goes down into the soil not beautiful but strong and hard. Like in Europe, the miracle of the underground, not of birds singing in trees, no, underground. A certain time of year, I said, God speaks in the furrow not in the perfume and blossom of flowers. I saw the startled happy face of the old man, his pipe forgotten. This is the day of descent I said into tomorrow. My brother did this and others, it takes millions of seed. Those who look to death, who do not give this seed into the dark, are ghosts of yesterday. My brother will live. I looked down at the faces, and bodies, in the heat. Everything, I said, will live in Man, and in those who mother and father him forth. I stopped and felt very foolish and I saw Steve with his hand stretched from below to me and I jumped down into the darkness of their shouts, applause and those who embraced me and put a hand on my shoulder and above all the eyes looking at me with happiness.

I hardly knew what happened after that. Many women moved near me. Steve was beside me. The old man seemed to be near. The lamb was roasted. The old warriors cut slices of rich juicy meat and as the sun went down we bit into the delicious smoky flesh. I did not want to leave ever. My sister looked anxious, thinking I was tired. "A little while longer," I said. "Please." Steve kept my hand in his. "Machine gun callouses," he laughed, showing me. The Lithuanians were counting the money from the lamb. . . . Slowly, sleepily, happily the people were all going home, the children hanging blissful and limp.

We heard singing from the barbecue grove and there sat the old lamb-eating warriors roasting a little beast on the hot fine coals, passing a bottle of strong white liquor and one began to hum.

They sang together many songs I had never heard, some slow and sad, some with marching anger and their women joined them and sometimes they sang together and some danced in the clearing and I had never heard anything like it, living so near and never known to us.

I said to Steve, "Who are they all over the earth?"

He smiled and nodded, singing a chorus. The old gnome was standing by the embers marking time with his pipe and I saw his long arms and the giant hands spatulate like living animals swinging from the boughs of his body, which looked as if it had been forged by Vulcan, hammered out.

"I will sing the song," he said, "together we will sing the chorus."

His voice was surprising from the great barrel of chest, pouring from the spigot, powerful and warm, and he seemed like a giant in the woods. Steve took my hand waiting for the chorus with pleasure and when it came he nodded and beat time with his head, smiling, pressing against me in the earth darkness.

And together we all sang the chorus.

Eroded Woman

The sight of the shanty in the lead mine district brought back many strains of melancholy from my childhood in Oklahoma, and it was as if I had always remembered the bare duned countryside and the tough, thin herb strains of men and women from the Indians of the Five Tribes to the lean migrants from Valley Forge. Standing before the shack, an old lean-to, pine bent and tense from the metal onslaught of sun, I was afraid to see the woman I knew would open the door.

The abandoned lead and zinc mines stand in a wasteland of ruined earth and human refuse. Ruin shows in the form of the shanty roof, in the shape of the awful knothole eye which admits chat-laden wind and light, in the loose swinging door. The insecurities of my childhood are awakened. The mine shaft openings glitter in the sunlight and the unreal day seems to shift and shatter and the old fear emanating from the land gnaws at me, fear of space, of moving, of the town, of what?

A union man in Joplin had told me to knock at this door. "The old lady is a fighter, her son is a fighter from way back! We had the blue-card company union here first. They played all the tricks, control of relief, goons, they even had armed Indians against strikers, called everybody furriner and Communist, but we got railroaders blacklisted far back as the '94 strike, and old miners from Little Egypt who knew the score. We held out. Now we got a union. You go see the old lady."

She answered my knock. She was spare, clad in a kind of flour sack with a hole cut in the middle, showing the hulk of her bones and also the peculiar shyness, tenderness and dignity of a woman who has borne children, been much alone, and is still strong set against rebuff.

She was shy and I was shy. When I told her who sent me she let me into the rickety house which seemed only an extension of her gothic body. She wiped a chair with her skirt. "Set," she said. "It's the chat, overn everything."

"You lived here long?"

She looked at me. Her eyes seemed dusted with chat, their blueness dimmed and yet wide open and upon me, magnets of another human being. "A sight of time," she

said, "too long. When we come we were always going
back to the Ozarks to a farm." We both looked out of the
crooked frame of the window. A chat pile rose up, there
was not a tree, flower or bush. "Nothing will ever grow,"
she said, fixing her gnarled, knucked hand in the flour sack
of her lap. "Seems like you're getting sludge in yore
blood."

We both looked out of the crooked window. More is
said in silence than in words. It is in silence that she trusts
me. "The Quapaws owned this land but the big oil scared
them and they signed it over for ninety-nine years. I guess
that's forever as us'n goes. I wouldn't sign over green land
like that to some critters I never see.

"My son will be here. He will tell you. He's thinking
all the time. Sometimes when he ain't working he makes
me nervous setting thar but I know now he's thinking it
out. Since the C.I.O. come here he's been thinking. Since
they had that row and we was all out of work for so long
and they broke up our meetings and they beat up my son.
They beat him bad and my husband didn't say anything
agin't. 'Ellie,' he said, 'he's fighting for his kin. He's
fighting good.' And I tended him for two weeks bandag-
ing his raw skin. His skin was peeled off'n him. Not an
inch but what was pounded like a steak and I never said
nothing to him. It looked like he was hurt for some reason
that was not just hurt like in the mines, not just death. It
makes you sore after awhile, no use seem to comin' of it.
Like all the babies born so hard and dying so early."

A young man came up the walk. "It's my son that
was in the strike," she said. "I been widowed twice. It's
the chat hemorrhage both times. You drown in your own
blood, you do. Hello, son," she said.

The boy was silent and shaggy, with the same blue
eyes and a tense grievance in him. He sat on the edge of the
bed, his cap in his hand. "Yes, we've got a union now,
right of our blood we have. They done everything to us."

"They beat him," she said softly looking at him, and
he looked fiercely and briefly at her.

"Yes, the Klan, the bosses, pickhandlers beat up every
man with a CIO button. The merchants give dances and
prizes if you belonged to the Blue Card."

"They tried to run him out, beat him up twice," she
said.

"Don't lower your voice. The Klan don't rule here
now, mamma," he said.

"I don't know. The Republicans are coming back. The Republicans sent the army. The army!" she said.

"Talk right up," he said.

"We would not give up fighting for the people and the land. I'm mighty proud of him not to lick the boots of the company. Now I'll be fixing the supper if you'll all excuse me."

When he got into it he was like a man in love. "Why," he said, "I'd kill a child of mine before he'd work in the mines. Children of lead, that's all we call them. I saw my father die, his lungs turned to stone, setting in that chair there till he held his breath and let his blood choke him and then he could lie down forever." Now the union was going to send him North to a school and he was going to learn. He didn't know anything. His mother would go with him and they would go North.

"Another migration," I said.

He looked at me. "You think we should stay? Stay put, eh?" He began to walk around the room, his hands in his pockets. The Mrs. came in. "Well," he said, "I got the seeds of unionism in me. My dad carried his union card in his heart for a long time, couldn't carry it nowheres else. He was always telling us a better life was coming through the union no matter how long we had to fight, he used to tell us. You can always do whatever you have to do to win."

The mother came to the door and said, "If you can eat what we eat, I guess like we used to say if we can stand it all year you can stand it for one meal."

We went into the lean-to kitchen. You could see the earth through the cracks but the boards were scrubbed clean as a butcher's table.

"I was a weaver back in Virginia," the mother said. "Why, if Mr. Baxter, the owner of the mill, was here this minute he could tell you, I could shore weave!"

The meal was a big plate of beans the color of dry locusts and some cornmeal bread. "If'n we had ketchup it would be tasty," he said. "Set!"

We bowed our heads. "Dear Lord, make us thankful fer what we are about to receive and fer all the blessing we receive at Thy hands. In Jesus name we ask it, amen."

The son wanted to tell what he knew. He believed at first that the blue-card union was the best because it "ain't furrin and it ain't Red" and you kept your job. Then the Blue Card had deliberately affiliated with the "furrin" union, the AF of L.

"A man don't know which way to turn. There was riot and killing in Galena. Lots of folks showed up here from all over. The Communists they help you and they ain't afeared. They call them furriners too."

"Henry," she laughed, "he says the whole darn district is getting furrin, he says he's gonna go on further West. Further West." They laughed.

She sang in a crooked voice, *"Ladies to the center, form a star, kill all furriners near and far.* We used to sing that. Don't never see how a union against the boss is always furrin. My man always was a union man and I don't always rightly understand but I am with him till the day I die and his thinking is my thinking and his way is mine. *Heigh ho, heigh ho, I joined the CIO, I give my dues to the goddamned Jews, heigh ho, heigh ho.* Not even a song like that got our boys to testify agin the CIO. They had to bring in a lot of wild boys and pay some drunk Indians to look like they was a big army agin the CIO. The pick-handle boys went around and the Klan come in."

"I got to be goin,'" the boy said.

"He's always off to a meeting," she said proudly.

He stopped at the door. "It's mighty fine, writing something. I hope you do it." He stood a moment. I held out my hand and he hesitated a moment in the dusky door, then in a rush he took it.

When he had gone it was dusk and the wood darkened. I said, "Don't light a lamp. It's nice to sit in the dusk."

"It's nice," she said sitting closer to me. "I should wash the dishes."

"I'll help you after a while. Let's just sit together." She was pleased.

I could feel the clearness of the woman, the edge, the honor, the gothic simplicity of the lean struggle and the clarity and honor with which she lived. She was close to the bone, her face honest as her house with the terrible nakedness of a tool, used as a tool is used, discarded as a tool, worked as a tool, uncared for as a human. And underneath there stirred the almost virginal delicate life of the woman, her modest delicate withdrawals, the bare and meager boundaries of her person kept intact, unviolated, with human tenderness emanating from her, like live energy. We sat close together.

"The long trek we been doin'. My children always thinkin' we are crossing a river or that the wind is on the wagon shaking and moving. We was movin' a lot. Why, we picked up everything when the mines open at Picher. Everyone was talking about a big lead and zinc vein over here, everybody was tearing out fer the new diggings jest across the line into Oklahoma, jest a hole in the road. It was a time I tell you when everybody was on the road. You see yore neighbor sticking his head outen his shack which was movin' comical right down the road and the living going on as usual, the kids hoppin' in and out shouting more'n usual. Farmers were a-coming from Arkansas and Alabama even and Tennessee scurrying like ants to a new corpse. Ozark hillbillies was comin' in on the freights, knocking on the door at night fer victuals, women even rode the blinds in with their children. Houses from Joplin carted, villages lifted right up and took on wheels, timber pulled by mules right onto the new diggins in Oklahoma.

"First we left the cotton hills, we come trying to git us'n a piece of land in Arkansas sharecropping, but we come on here in the night then when a friend comin' through in a covered wagon with his family and said he is going to Galena for to work in the zinc thar. I didn't want my man to work ever again under the earth but he telling me then he says, No, Elly, you kin make a stake thar, we ain't aimin' to stay thar at all. We aimin' to make a little stake and then we goin' into that new territory of Oklahoma we stayin' thar, he says.

"We got us some of that land, that new good land and raisin' a crop of kids and whatever they are raisin' in them parts, but it's good land. That thar was years ago afore the twins died and layin' out thar in no proper earth I think sometimes I hear them playing in the woodshed. Now back in Kentucky, I recollect thar was good sweet earth with the sweet rot of leaves and it's just I think I hear them. I know I don't really hear them."

All of her teeth had gone, she said, by her fourth baby and her chin grew upward around as if to protect the sunken mouth and cheeks. "My man got as clever a turn as you want to see with everything. I got no education at all. We got one book, a hymn book. I know the words and I point them out to my sons a long time afore he knew I couldn't read a scratch. I was ashamed. I never felt much like larnin' when I come from the mill. My pa was for larnin'. He said, you don't know, you air shut up. My ma couldn't read but she knew more'n any living woman I ever heard tell of. And when pa was kilt in the mill she

worked as hard fer her family as cunning and strong you
had to be. Born in Catawba County, her pa owned a farm
there afore the rebel war. He never owned a slave and was
bitter agin it saying the white man and the black man had
to stand together, but all his sons was killed in it one way
or another and it don't seem fair.

"Funny thing, the men always dyin' early. Hard life
and dangerous, in my family the women is left with all the
chilluns to raise and by that time you sure ain't in no shape
to get another man.

"I remember we had beds of white maple pa made.
Then he was one with his hands but hard times done us out
of them, we sold them for quite a fancy price I remember.
Pa worked in the field and raised a good part of what we
et. We drawed ten cents a day in the mill. Ma drawed
twenty-five. It were winter time when I begun to work. I
recollect we went to work by lantern light and the kerosene
lamps swinging away in the ceiling I thought they was some
kind of bugs swinging away there. Then my brother went
to the mill, four of us drawing money. Hard times fer us,
hard fer me. I got a fever I recollect, takes grit to get a
body along. I just got over the typhoid and I went to the
boss and I says I'm wuth more'n ten cents a day. I was a
shy body I just didn't think I had nothin to lose we
couldn't eat with four of us working and he raised me to
twenty cents and told me not to tell nobody.

"Do you think I'll meet them all in heaven? Do you
believe they will be there now? I remember them all. Sadie,
Goldie, Elijah, all of them and some of the dead ones more
than the living. Oh, how it goes on and how you live
through it! Claire, Kate and the dogs and cats and mules
and cows and calves I have fed, always feeding something,
day and midnight trying to get something to eat.

"I mourned and always mourn. Here was the pasture
land and cows grazing and the green land I remember and
crickets and in no time quicker than scat the green pasture
was turned over like the palm of my hand and the mills was
belching at the tailings and the gray chat begin to drift in
all the cracks and the green land was agone forever agone
and never coming back in our time."

She arose shyly. White in the gloom, the match struck
sharp in her knuckled tree-bark weaver's hands. She held
it, shaking a little, to the lamp wick. The light shook, distended like an eye, and the house sprang in the night in the

ruined land. I saw the awkward, hunted, lost and wild endurance of her strong odored herb body which I could smell like night herb and I wanted to reach out and touch her but knew her flight. The door hung crooked outward and she went to close it. I saw the darkness, like an eye, through a knot hole of the bleached skeletal sun-wracked pine — a thin boat in the night on a vacant sea. I saw the frail, sagging iron bed. The broken mirror held the light in a sharp rectangle. She was looking steadily at me, holding me in her silence. I saw a picture of a dead child. A picture of a bride and groom in a round frame, a garland of paper, faded roses about it.

I felt her deep exhaustion and her sorrow, wakened and warmed by unaccustomed talking, like soil stirred, the sorrow of its ruin reflected in her, the human and the land interlocked like doomed lovers.

I felt a kind of anguish as if we rode a Moby Dick of terror — as if a great beast rode under us not of earth but of a ruthless power that we could neither see nor call by name.

Her eyes in ambush look out at me for what I am thinking, gravely watchful. "My son will stay with a friend, if you would not mind to sleep with me."

I lay awake thinking of human waste, of injuries which reflect on the indifference and callousness of us all, of the unrecorded lives of dead children, the million-faceted darkness of their fear and sorrow like my own of being trapped far below ground in American life.

All over mid-America now lamplight reveals the old earth, reveals the story of water, and the sound of water in the darkness repeats the myth and legends of old struggles. The fields lie there, the plow handles wet, standing useless in the mud, the countless seeds, the little houses, the big houses, the vast spider network of us all in the womb of history, looking fearful, not knowing at this moment the strength, doubting the strength, often fearful of giant menace, fearful of peculiar strains and wild boar power and small eyes of the fox.

The lower continent underlying all speaks below us, the gulf, the black old land.

Summer Idyl, 1949

Every spring the water pours off the land like sorrow from the deforested regions where the tall trees no longer hold moisture in their roots and the suitcase farmers have plowed under more land for bonanza wheat harvests. It is the same this year. The buses detour, the land is eroded, the midwest Chamber of Commerce organizes against the Missouri Valley Authority.

When you start going west it is the most morning morning of the world, the sunlight in front of you, the shouts of morning lying over the green world, the flat wheat and dairy land stretching ahead, the valleys rising and rolling like squalls at sea. There she lies, the earth and her people growing the wheat for which the world hungers. The bus whizzes through Main Street, beginning and ending on the prairie, past the old men on the courthouse steps, the ample mothers and beflowered young girls and the prairie wantons. The sight of the countryside to those who live close to it is as immediate as touch, as love, and pain and time of the past, undulating to Cambrian horizons like tremendous ghosts, the corn hills of the Sioux, totemic communal effigies in the green declivities, our own ghost towns, forgotten villages of our birth become prophecies of a future, fears of your own body, your own hunger projected, your skeleton foretold.

A country can die as a man and woman can. It can become strange as a corpse and full of decay and your mind can dissolve in fear without a sound like a stone dropped in water, sinking. You can all look strange to each other, immersed in fright, immobilized in the hidden flood accumulating and surfacing.

The river was rising and the bus would be held up. There was that genius of communal warmth which, sadly, in American life is invoked only by disaster, when some kind of reality and love rises like a submerged and magic ship. At the trailer camp a lean man walks back and forth, sniffing the air, runs his car radio, listening to the river and highway patrols. His face twitches, he cracks his knuckles, his eyes are unfocused as if, as they say in Kansas, he had an eye out east and west for cyclones. "Awful," he says, "Won't get through till morning. Terrible. To be stopped by a river. I'm a self-made man and a river can't stop me. Thought I could beat the river but failed. Held up twenty-four hours. Got to get there tonight. I just made a bet I'd get there."

"Who did you bet with?" I ask.

"With myself," and when I ask him if he has important business at his destination, he says he has no business there and doesn't know a soul and just bet with himself....

I visit the tavern in the corn field. Inside there is a great bar with dark cooled air, fragrant with women and liquor. You see these now all over the midwest, in the countryside, with a curtained upstairs and below the corn, tunneled under, gambling rooms with glass and chromium. In this underground labyrinth below the corn roots much money changes hands, and city machines far away are enriched in corruption. The hub of the mineral and agricultural country feeds the capitalist horse and is not even enriched by its droppings in return.

It is startling to move from the bright sunny afternoon to the smoky dark, reflected in the many mirrors, and mysteriously upon you are invisible eyes as if down the barrel of a gun, asking who you are. As I sat on the bar stool a flash of sympathy passed between me and a blonde girl at one of the tables who was talking to two men. She has a delicate face that suggests frailty if not illness. "Look at me," the older man is saying to her. "My nerves is frayed out. I ain't an old man. I ain't as young as you," he says bitterly to the other, a young man, thin as a grasshopper, with a mouth like one, a sharp slit tongue as his mind leaps lasciviously from one excitement to another, unsavory lusts, appetites, rumors, which make him vicious as a mad locust. "I tell you," the thin man says, leaning across the girl who rears away from him, "It's the Jews. Roosevelt was a Jew. The Communists are Jews. Hitler was OK on the Jews, maybe he went a little too far maybe he didn't."

"I suppose the Poles and the Irish are Jews too," the girl laughs, tossing her delicate head, "Oh the fox is on the town." She looks at me and laughs and shakes her head toward some invisible and ironic god. They both press upon her like vultures — how about it honey how about a time tonight huh? She says, "I got some big stuff tonight not with the little foxes and you better not let Al see you. They ordered half a dozen blondes and half a dozen brunettes at the big house tonight."

The grasshopper whistles, "Meat order. Say I wish
you'd get me in with those big boys. They're gonna stop
communism all right. I went to a meeting in K.C., a secret
meeting. They aren't sleeping, the big boys. String along
with me honey. I'm gonna take them. I'm all jacked up
about the future."

She tells him what he can do with his future, and
comes over and sits beside me on a stool and I order a
drink for her and she tells me she was a school teacher,
has a child, sings at night here in the tavern, has a boy
friend, Al, who will come to take her to the "Big House,"
and who is in the big house, oh — big gang stuff they pay
twenty-five an evening, order so many blondes, so many
brunettes when they entertain, got a country estate that
would knock your eyes off, old prohibition gangs now own
the countryside, bought up her dad's farm too, two of her
brothers died in the war and she's glad they're dead. She is
interested in writing, if she could write what she knows and
somebody would print it, it would be plenty! She says
maybe she could take me along as a friend, if Al is willing.
After two more drinks and some more badinage with the
two salesmen, and some other girls had gathered at one of
the tables with make-up kits, a horn outside announced Al
and I followed them out.

"A friend of my mother's," she said to Al. "You
know I thought while we wait for the act we could talk."
He didn't answer, but he didn't say no and she gave me an
ironic wink and I got in beside her and the other girls got in
back and Al drove like a bat out of hell all the time with a
trigger finger touching Bernice's thigh until he let out a
howl and she said coldly so my skin prickled, "This pin
goes in about four inches to the hilt."

We came to a big sign which said "Farms
Incorporated," drove through an iron gate not connected
with any fence and up to a mansion set in the woods and Al
drove to the rear and we all got out and went through a kitchen crowded with cooks and waiters and mounds of
shrimp and chicken and a whole roasted pig on the table
and barbecue spits beginning to move. I went with the
girls. Most of them worked at other jobs during the day,
did this at night "when they could get it." The whole place
was sinister and for reasons one could not name was full of
violence and fear. "I hate these people," Bernice said
close to me with her curious clairvoyance for what you

were thinking. "Pigs, swine," she said. "You don't know. They save us for the stunt."

I could hear laughter from the house. We all sat depressed, some of the girls slept . . . Bernice talked to me as if a river in flood, as if she told me in the small time her whole life. We ate dinner brought in on rolling tables, turkey plates, and the girls ate ravenously. The place was lighted, the voice of men, music came from the front of the house, big shiny cars were parked in a lot to the side, outdoor lights went on over a great swimming pool and Bernice told me to go through the poplars, not be seen by anyone, stand at the end of the pool in a driveway there and Al would pick us both up afterwards.

An invisible orchestra began to play and I stood in amazement. In the middle of the pool a huge lotus opened and inside the five brunettes stood picked out in the roving spots. They were naked and after dancing plunged into the water. There was laughter as one of the guests fully dressed jumped in after them.

I was grabbed from behind and my arms vised to my sides and held and then Al's voice said, "Oh it's mother's friend." "You're pretty strong, Al," I said, "Where did you take your training?" "I been a pretty good fighter," he said, "ain't so bad yet. More money in this stuff." I asked him what stuff was that but he shut up and I said I'd never seen so much food in my life and he said that was nothing this was a small party, I should have seen the fowls frozen with roses and live goldfish and the whole steers cooked in wine. "That's my boss, everything up brown . . . when he gives he gives plenty, thousands of pheasants, frozen shad, I tell you this is something big, bigger than you know, and I'm in on it. I seen checks. I could tell plenty."

"If he's so big why can't you tell me his name?"

"Don't be nosy, mama's friend, it'll come out in time. . . . Here they come."

Into the light, chased by drunken men, ran a flock of naked girls. The light picked them out going in and out in the shadow and sometimes they cried out and the drunken cries of the men mingled with the music. Then I saw that the drunken men had sling shots and pockets full of stones and they stopped and aimed at the running girls. Some circled back, fell to the ground under the hunters. The lights played in long streamers on this incredible scene. I saw Bernice running towards us, circling wide into the shadow

of the tall trees. She ran swift with that strange tenacious
energy in her now alive to escape. Al got a cloak and
waited to fling it around her and a voice, cracked and
strange, called like a monstrous baby — "Honey honey let
me find you." It was worse than some bestiality, that high
feminine voice, and then the fat blind drunk face pierced
by light, the queer sling shot in his hand. Bernice shivered
in the cloak and I felt ashamed of my own fear seeing that
she was laughing and her teeth shaking, and that she did
not hold fear but the instinct and health of the history and
the country from which she came, and lived, and slowly
died.

   We ran to the car, Al threw it in gear and tore out with
that violent way in which he drove, and we flew through
the countryside into the breasted hills that I could tell were
still warm from the day and spoke of hiding places of
strength and maternal curve against a sky strangely lighted
as if from some burning city. Bernice snuggled into the
bandit protection of Al and she turned in the dark, her
small face white and the fearful eyes big. "I play and sing
at the tavern." "Gee you sure got union hours," I said.

   I shouldn't have said it. Al looked at me suspiciously.
"I'm gonna send my boy to college." "College," Al
snorted. "Yeah, college," she said. "Ain't no need of
college by the time he's gone to his first whore." She
pulled away from him, her anger like a whip against me.
"Your friends ain't gonna have it your way, not by a long
shot, not at all." "Shut up," he said looking at me suddenly as if he had done wrong to take me. Bernice leaned
my way and began to laugh and Al slammed on the brakes
as we pulled into the tavern gravel. When Bernice didn't
stop laughing he slugged her at the nape of the neck so she
fell over the wheel as he got out and slammed the door. She
shook herself like a cat. "Forget it," she said. "Want to
catch the show? I'm the Mildred Bailey of the Border."

   "Maybe I shouldn't go in," I said.

   "Oh Al? Don't let him scare you," she said. I went in
and saw the young men two deep at the bar, without
women, waiting for her. There were several amputees
from the last war. They clapped, formed a pool around
her in a curious impersonal mass lust, and she rose on the
platform in the light, with the polished glass and bottles
aglitter around her, adjusted the heavy accordion, flour-
ished and chorded with that flow of steel strength in her
and she sang to the young men of the double cross, the

giant in the mountain, in the heart, chained, weeping, tortured, no one speaking of him except in covert weeping, in the shadow, in the obscured and broken word. Something hidden and emerging as violence and cruelty creeps in the song and the young men listening, the money world holding them off from even tragedy, and the smell of carnage smelling sweet as lavender proclaiming that we have friends who tell us, but really Lazarus, rising stenched from the mortgaged land, from the house made a phantom by absentee owners who suck blood from afar, from neat sell-outs and atomic explosions in distant lands and dead we never count.

A country can die as a woman can . . . I touch her shoulder and she turns from the young men, her cornsilk hair belling and her eyes starting alive toward me, her hands upon me and the haunting and clinging of the asking upon my flesh. "I'll see you again," she says holding me, "I'll surely see you again. Come back again. You must come back." Through the smoke I saw her watching me to the door and I felt the eyes of Al and the other eyes down the barrel of a gun. I turned to face all the hatred, and the eye of bouncer and stool and bodyguard and raised my hand and she gave me a curious nod, throwing her head back in that satiric salute and defiance.

Back in the trailer camp my nervous betting friend was still cracking his knuckles and I suggested we go out and see them get the cattle out of the lowlands. It was dark and the night was fragrant and full of flood menace and men working happily together in disaster. We came quickly to the blocked road and beyond the drama of isolated farm houses, floundered heifers rescued, boats full of squealing pigs. Trucks piled up on the road and some slept in the marooned cars or played cars or sang or made love and some others were selling sandwiches and peddling anything they could buy up cheap. On the edge of the flood a little old tavern stood on stilts used and prepared for water, and now full of men and juke box muxic and my friend was very nervous until he asked a patrol cop what to do and we went into the tavern, flavorsome of men, beer fumes and that intangible and wonderful sudden blooming excitement always emerging in our life in disaster. A glow rose and emanated communally, shone on every face brightening from the swamps of its own despair, and for the moment a common danger was like a campfire in a freezing prairie, in which they stood illumined, welded from separateness to communal warmth and mutual aid, for the moment freely aiding each other without prejudice or fear or remuneration.

The farm men and boys, still burnt from corn planting, beards and eyes bright with fatigue and excitement, some of them with no sleep for nights, told many a tale as the bartender filled the glasses and bottles popped and secret moon came out of pockets. The railroad men in their blue-billed caps were there because trains were stalled behind the flood.

"I'm going down to see them get the cows out of the swamp and they say a woman is marooned on top of an outhouse. I can skirt around. I see like a cat in the dark." The fear and anxiety flicked across him like a cat o' nine tails, and as I knew he would, he said he'd wait, and he called after me that he'd make a bet with himself that I'd be back in half an hour.

I stepped off the highway and into the fragrant moist and terrible darkness. I was frightened, alert and excited. In five minutes I might have been on wilderness road full of the shouts of men, the grunting of animals, the baying of dogs and the labial sound of water. Animals fled and birds moved in the thicket and owls flew over the bottom land.

I came through a thicket and could see a light rotating across the water which was black as flint, and it struck the green signals of drowned corn. The light I saw was from a small row boat where two men crouched and illumined a woman with her arms lifted, wild, upon a floating outhouse, tipped crazily as it strained from some snag and she lurched upon it in song, raising and lowering her arms, as she cried and prayed in a powerful hog-caller's voice, as she cried unto the Lord from Mount Outhouse and the men were a little tickled and awed.

"Millie, do you hear?" one of the men in the boat shouted through his cupped hands and she answered, "I hear the voice of God. I am safe in the arms of Jesus."

"Well, why not leave her? Her old man has been dead four years."

"Shut up and pull that rope tighter. I can lasso her down. She weighs as much as a brood sow. Shut up and row."

I was startled by a man's shout almost upon me and I saw rearing in the dark the frightened faces of bellowing cows as he drove them up onto the levee and in a frenzy the unseen shouting man bellowed steadily, screamed and beat their rumps, keeping them from committing suicide in the moiling water. He came into the play of searchlight, pulled back to the ground against a roped tug of a heifer. He was parallel with the ground as he pulled them up the levee, and I could hear the terror and struggle of man and beast in the water.

A kind of primeval fear made me turn back. I could see the glow of the tavern neon and I stepped into a bog to my knees in real panic and felt caught as if by the suction of hands and at the same time I heard an awful sound that froze my blood. Like a hundred women screaming, it ripped the night. I saw then, as I pulled my legs out of the bog, a farm house on higher ground and a small light from one of the windows and the screams seemed to come from there. I made for higher ground and the house and perhaps there would be a fire, and perhaps someone was in pain, hurt — the cries came strangely like cries in child-birth. I looked in the window before going to the door. A dim flashlight, which someone had tied with a kerchief to keep it focused, threw a light from the floor, adding to the terror of the scene.

It was a big abandoned farm kitchen literally alive with frightened rabbits which had sought refuge there from the flood. Two young men with bloody naked torsos shouted from ferocious faces and ran the rabbits into corners where they clubbed them, then slit the skin from stem to stern, skinned the coats off them and threw them into a pot steaming on an old stove. The rabbits ran toward the light, turned and seemed to look at me just before the blow struck them between the lily cavity of ear and the round eye pooled with fear.

I turned and ran back into the swamp, away from the yelling men, the praying women, the grunting animals and was emitted onto the road almost instantly and the cars still lined against the flood and my friend with his watch open. . . . "Holy Mackerel," he said. "Thirty minutes to the dot. Who won? What did you see?"

"Flood," I gasped. "Flood." I could not speak of the sudden brutality, heroism, despair and *something* that stands often speechless, eyeless, behind our life, the cry, the club, the flood.

The fly cop tells my nervous friend, still cracking his
knuckles, that you may be able to make it through now on
another highway. He asks me to drive through with him.
It's somebody to bet with anyhow. We drive into the
flood. There is still a road that is not yet covered. He
drives like mad, as if pursued by a thousand devils. He is
excited. We'll make it, he keeps saying. We'll surely make
it. We get to the broad meadow land, now covered with
water, but men are working with sandbags and markers
have been put along each side so you won't drive off the
road, and you can still go through. . . . A tall young man
solemnly signals us to drive on.

"Hello," says a man sticking his head in the window.
He has a strong Indian face, and the excitement of working
all night, of battling with others against a river. That night
at least he has been a part of a struggle with others.

"How is it?" I ask.

"Good." He flashes white teeth. "You're just in the
nick. I'll clear the way, I know this road like my hand.
Take it easy. Good. Good. Water comes to the hubs we'll
make it. . . . I'll just see you across."

The men along the way stand knee-deep in water,
saluting, shouting down the flood.

American Bus

All day the bus has whizzed through Main Streets beginning and ending abruptly at the prairie, past the old men sitting in the green sun on courthouse steps, out of the winter shadow. Out the bus window you see the tractors and sometimes horses plowing. A man at noon squatted at the end of a field, the color of the soil that had blown on him. Horses fly along beside the bus like porpoises at sea, the light striking through their outflung tails and manes.

All along at whistle stops, crossroads, villages there is the cry, bustle and beauty of the prairie women, bursting out in spring finery; the young girls brightly dressed, the matrons happily bedecked and curled like temple dancers. There are women whose laughter tells of the wonders of spring hay rides, barn dances and evening doings, nocturnal cries and strange lights from the village cemetery where the dead have tolerance for the young going to a bad war.

The women carry life upon them like the bee does pollen. The sight of the countryside to them is not pictorial, but touch and hunger and work and love. They live upon the old Cambrian sandstone alive and vigorous. They talk of spelling bees, county fairs, the Last Man's Club, Kiwanis, singing contests, funerals, the canning factory, the mysterious factory that just came to the village and that everyone thinks is making some part of a gun. And most of all they talk of the war, of dead sons, of living sons going west into a terrible darkness. One says: "It's getting nowadays the parents bury the children instead of the children burying the parents. When that happens a civilization is falling, falling."

I listen to the conversation, imbibing the rich day and night talk of the countryside, the quick knowing of the earth and the machine. Yet the old American fear strikes into me and I feel a sense of doom and wretchedness so I can hardly breathe. I see our people so strong, so tough and fey, so keen, quick, accurate, so humorous, full of whimsy, fantasy, prankishness, such inside-out prairie waifs, so strong and enduring, yet often turned ugly, living high upon the death of brothers, plowing deep into the earth, into the flesh of their fathers, pulling up as bones the substance of man's hope. When I was a child on long migrations I was afraid.

I am afraid now, but I have a light and a compass.

The young, tired, worn-out truck drivers who drive cars and machinery a long distance from the factory, then ride back to sleep, carouse three days, then go on the grind again, are talking and sharing a bottle of whiskey, which is the only thing that keeps you alive in the loneliness. There is a thin one named Pee Wee with fright in his eye and a better one named Butch, who knows what it's all about or thinks he does. He says:

"Anything but being alone. I hate to be alone. Speakin' of this country — and nobody was — well, you know you can't never tell what's gonna happen. Nobody does. You make it up, see? Bungle along, see? I even invented a draft to a stove once, didn't know what I was doin', just made it the hard way from one minute to the next and bingo — there I had an invention. It's all rigged."

"It's rigged, all right," Pee Wee said. "You take them unions."

Butch exploded and I could see his fine busted face, the nose wangled sideways in his Golden Glove days, his whole face as well as his chain drive, solid Mack jargon, full of strains, whimsy, violence, batting averages and heroic losses.

"Union," he shouted, "let me tell you, boy, you're talking from pure unashamed ignorance. Let me tell you you never took one of those big babies out on the road at a twenty-hour stretch like we used to do for twenty-two bucks a week if you got it and *if* you got into home plate alive. Those big trailers used to be piled up like kindling and the guy trapped inside burning and the blow torches doing him no good. I could tell you we was killing each other off, big loads, cutting in. Excuse me, brother, don't talk to me about unions. Now it's all in the contract, that's it, whether you can be a human being, get some sleep, have a girl, no longer a fly-by-nighter. It's all in the contract and if you tear it up you go back to being a slave screamin' your guts out."

He told how the contract was about hours, wages, run-time, eating, getting paid.

Pee Wee said finally: "You would not be driving a truck if you'd read the books I do about getting ahead." Butch snorted at this — where would he want to get?

Everybody becoming a leader was hooey. Who'd want it and how would you do it anyway?

"Magnetize yourself," says the tiny Pee Wee, and I thought Butch would explode. Pee Wee emboldened by the bottle, is infatuated with the wonders of power. "Get whatever you want, get ahead, do the Extra Mile. Many men started as poor boys and became millionaires. Have an inner drive, want to climb *higher*. Draw other people out in Tactful Conversation. You turn the telescope around so that you seem bigger and others smaller. Act like a *big* man. Don't lean against things, or lounge down in a chair and feel sick and out of it."

"I don't get it," Butch said laughing silently. "First you get yourself screwed up, try to step on everybody's face. Then you relax, take a nap while socking the guy above you — why you're working yourself up to an extreme state of poverty!"

I saw Pee Wee sitting up straight, not slouching, in his little terrible courage; and Butch's wild broken face, laughing, thrusting his head sideways, pity and laughter in his bent, socked, heroic face. "It's rigged, all right, you can say that again. I'll be alive all right, dang tootin', in the year A.B. 20. What's that? That's Atom Bomb the year 20."

They both seemed to fall asleep like dropping through a trap door.

He was a small man and when he got on the bus he looked around quickly, sat down beside me, pulled his neck in his collar. When we passed the big chromium taverns sitting in the corn fields, I said that they must represent the spread of Al Capone out over the prairie. Leaning close to me, he began to talk, his hand over his mouth: "It's happening," he said. "I'm leaving Wisconsin. You know why? First there was O'Konski and now there's McCarthy, and the son of old Bob LaFollette has to shoot himself straight through the head. It's happening."

Terror was like a musk coming from his skin, and his eyes darted like a ferret. "I'm a refugee," he said again. "I'm going down South, see if I can get a business. In my home town you can't associate with anyone. We used to be liberal. Now everyone is afraid to think. I don't want to be there anymore. Carnival men, crooks, gangsters telling you how to vote, yelling the Big Lie. The old Capone gang, an octopus moving out into the countryside controlling everything, insects in the corn kernel. I've seen it before.

"A shakedown, that's what it is. First I paid a little gangster, but now the big gangster I will not pay. I'd be afraid to tell everything. Somebody might be listening. Am I speaking low? Bawdy houses, gaming, politics, city machines, labor unions, big business and now war all mixed up. Cesspools of the city spilling into the country."

The bus stops and he stops talking. We have gone a few miles when he leans over, he must tell me: "I got out of Germany too. Just in time. I'm a Jew."

The Mexican woman in the rest room where we stop for lunch bends down, resting in balance, the round sun-ripe globe of her breast held between her fingers as she offers it to the baby, while I hold the little girl. She is glad to spill some of the pressure of her long trek now after working in beets, wheat, peas, corn, shacking all winter in a miserable hovel. She is trying to get to the new Dakota oil fields where her man is. She speaks of the field work:

"It is good pay: sometimes fifty cents an hour, once seventy-five, but we do not live by the hour. We live and eat every day, every week and the rains fall often." She means that when the rains fall, you do not work, but you are still hungry. "In peas," she says, "there is only a few hours to harvest before they spoil. A hot day comes, peas go up in smoke. Good weather work twenty-four hours. When good Roosevelt alive, we had good things, camps, even showers, and a paper with Government, so had to give you your pay. But all gone now. Gone with the good man. Gone. Camps closed now."

She tells how they came in the trucks from Texas standing tight like cattle, the driver getting fifteen dollars a head for each one arriving alive. "The children cannot learn, too much traveling. The baby is thin. Worry and your milk goes. I worked twenty-nine hours in the corn pack the day before this little one came. Even a mule couldn't stand that. We die, we live and the fields are waiting. We live and we move on the long distance and the rains fall often."

Driving towards the westering sun there are jokes, stories. A splendid old man gets on toward evening and sits with Pee Wee and Butch and they pass him the bottle. He is strong, a fringe of white hair, a ruddy sweet face. He

and tried to isolate him from his people through fear and intimidation of the Negro community.

He fought hard. And almost alone. And he kept breathing as long as he could, and kept fighting. And when he died from the heart he got in World War I, in a Jim Crow army, he died in the midst of Rondo, among his people, with the FBI patrolling the streets. It was clear at his funeral that the very death and body of this man could light a community and penetrate the bars of the "cage."

It was the week before Christmas. He lay in the white wooden house made into an undertaking parlor in the center of the "cage." He looked a young man, full of vigor, huge, with his eroded face that always reminded me of the exploited, suffering plowed black earth, filled out, the late ravages gentled over, his huge black hands folded. Who would dare come? Cars parked across the street contained the perpetual two, blond, arrow collar, large, well-fed on the people's tax money McCarthy twins familiar to us all. the undertaker was nervous. There were flowers from the many organizations Bill was part of; and at the last minute when one of his friends had said, if there are no flowers from the Party then there are no flowers at all, so at the door there stood a great spray of red roses with a note — "From the Communist Party of Minnesota." A woman who could not go said, "Bring me one of those roses, you know from which spray, so I can keep it."

The sun is pale, cold, and there are not many there. We couldn't get a singer so we have the record "We Shall Overcome Someday." You cannot help feeling the awful fright of this invisible tightening noose in this invisible cage within the gay December city. Some of the youth come — although many are working. One of them says, "I hope I'm not late to Bill's meeting." He looks down at the great sleeping face. He grins, "I never was at a meeting before where Bill didn't speak."

We did not know then how his life would speak in that day.

I went up to the corner and then I began to feel it. The whole community. It seemed alive behind the windows, around the corners, in some intelligence of the eye that looked straight at you, in two young men who looked anxiously towards the funeral house and followed me into the corner store which was full of youth, Negro youth, and I began to recognize them — from past struggles, meetings,

the picket line against Jim Crow at one of the popular
dance places, a thousand chance and fragmentary meetings, and without word or gesture my fear was dissipated,
gone. I understood they would not come, that they would
keep their own vigils. Outside, two women seemed by accident to drift down the street, to press my hand to say maybe they would come at my urging, but I understood they
expressed a fragment of a monumental ceremony which
was taking place, that the attendance in that small white
sarcophagus would be no measure of.

I cannot say with what physical prescience this living
strength was passed to me, almost with the strength of a
blow, and in silence. But I walked back no longer a frightened chip in the cold wind but part of a community. I real-
ized how much Bill taught all of us about the Negro. He
gently and firmly led us from chauvinism; he was a living
example of the strength of the weave of "black and white
together."

The funeral parlor is now full and more coming and it
seems to me there are many people who walk by on both
sides of the street past the two parked cars and the
McCarthy twins. They seem to just slowly walk by, many
of them, and some do not even look at the white wooden
house. They seem to pass ceaselessly.

An old friend of Bill's, a Negro minister, is going to
preside. They did not always agree, he tells me, but they
agreed on one thing, and that was the inevitability of
death. The undertaker tells how we must hurry through.
He is nervous. But the minister is an easy man and he
seems calm as we make out the "agenda." "Now Bill," he
said, "was an old friend of mine, we were in the Pullman
porters' strike together. He was a forerunner." "Say
that," I suggest, and he looks down at me gently. "Don't
hold out any hopes for my speech. I don't know what I'm
going to say." I don't believe he did. He was putting
himself out as tinder, waiting to catch the fire struck,
which he did so magnificently.

The "meeting" for Bill began, and the minister spoke
of his birth in Arkansas of slave grandparents, his mother
dying when he was thirteen. He set out North and there
learned to live in cities. In the world of gambling, quick
money, he wandered in that underworld of Capitalism. He
joined the church, searching. He became a worker. He got
angry at his boss. He got angry at chauvinism. "I used to
bleed at the eyes with hate," he said. And bragging at a

pool hall one day about how he'd told the boss off, the owner laughed at him — and he began to learn how to "organize his hate," he always said.

Then it seemed Bill took charge of his own "meeting." It began to happen. The first speaker is a beloved Negro leader, fighter with Bill in the early days in the struggle of the sleeping car porters. "Bill Herron," he says, "was a man of a new kind. Born in a slave family, he was a man who opposed the great kings of our time, the railroad kings, the steel kings. And at that time there was no protection, it was not a popular cause, nobody cared about the Pullman Porters but here was a man who fearlessly met power, and the great union of the Brotherhood of Pullman Porters attests to the fact that great power can be brought down by courage like this man had and belief in the united struggle of the people."

Then a young girl read a statement from the youth. She would rush off to the factory to get there at three. "Not only will we never forget Bill, the Negro and white youth, but we will never forget the things that made him special to us — his crossing a room to reach out his hand to one of us or putting his hand on our shoulder — 'You are growing up, becoming a man, the right kind of a man, the kind our people need.' Yes, each of us felt he was special because he had a special feeling for all of us. Bill is gone now but the things he taught us — that there can and will be a better world and the picture of a sterling man who was fighting until he died for what he knew to be good and right — will be with us. . . . The younger people, Negro and white, who knew Bill in St. Paul, Milwaukee, Minneapolis and Chicago and everywhere Bill lived, worked, and was active for peace in the world and equality for all peoples, will shed tears because we loved him. But we will pay the debt we owe him by seeing that peace, love and plenty for all in this world will replace greed, war and strife. That is what Bill would have wanted."

Then I spoke of Bill as teacher, brother, friend, comrade in struggle, born at the beginning of the span of the century, of the growth of the big monopolies and how at the end of his life I took him news every week and he rejoiced at the heroic struggles of the Chinese people, the people of India, Viet Nam, Africa and the struggle of his people in the Harlems of Milwaukee and Chicago, and how the freeing of Harold Ward of Chicago was one of the

last struggles in which he participated. I told about how
Bill wore a St. Paul street upon each foot — how he led us
in the Depression days — how he pounded the table of all
authority demanding that we eat. He was there where
there was a cry out, teaching us to use our strength and
pool our anger. He faced the Jim Crow of the Ambas-
sador Hotel in Washington, D.C., and broke it. and the
guns of General MacArthur and Mr. Hoover at the Bonus
March. He was a man like the Maccabees, like Jesus of
Nazareth who stood against the tax collectors, like
Toussaint L'Ouverture who stopped the armies of
Napoleon, like the leaders of the slave revolts in the tradi-
tion of Frederick Douglass, Ben Davis, Paul Robeson.

Then there began to be "amens," and outside the
window, slowly and ceaseless people seemed to be casually
walking by, as if the small wooden house had become the
hub of the hive, central to a hiving energy that seemed defenseless but was fierce and protective.

Now the Minister rises and his speech has been forged
and he launches it on a great sentence:
"Bill Herron was a man of a different kind, he was a man
    of a different kind, he was a man like Job, of his be-
    liefs. He was a man of this time, this place, on this
    earth.
He wanted no heaven in the future. Bill wanted no
    maybes.
He wanted it now, on this earth, in this place for all.
He was a man had no goods of this world.
He was a man like Job.
They told him give up your beliefs, curse God and die.
But he would not.
Covered with boils, sickened unto death, followed, still he
    believed.
You could not buy or sell him.
You could not make him crawl.
You could not break him . . . or frighten him, or silence
    him.
This man stood solid, straight, I couldn't go all the way
    with him but he was a man to be beside you. He was a
    man stood in this place, in this physical world against
    these forces now.
I first knew Bill when we were young men then in Montana
    in the porters strike and he walked up and down in
    front of the guns, and he defied the injunctions, and

he spit upon the big railroad bosses, and he said, *come on I'll be waiting for you*, and then it was not a recognized thing, not a known thing to fight for Negro porters, yes, my brothers and friends, the whole nation and the whole world was not supporting you then.

He stood a man before his time.

Now many men stand where he stood alone.

A crowd, a multitude will stand where Bill Herron stood with a few.

Jesus stood with a few, twelve men.

There are more here today and we know that those who came are marked down, Judases watch. Every man took a risk to come here.

So did they on the night they took Jesus from the cross.

The soldiers stood without. Only a few went to the hill and Herod's men watched in the night. If they were here, who want to come, the street would be packed block upon block.

This is a big crowd, of brave men and women, and we need those who stand up fearless like St. Paul, and Job and Jesus and Bill Herron.

Be not afraid.''

And no one was afraid.

He went on to give pictures of Bill's deep life in the Rondo district, so you knew why he came back there to die and to have his last meeting there. ''Sometimes,'' the minister said, ''you started to look for Bill, you needed to find him and you didn't have to look long or deep,'' he said, ''but you could most always find him. So last summer he said, he parked his car along a main street in Rondo and waited for Bill to come by, or word of him, and sure enough pretty soon he came out of a house right there, and stood on the porch for air, looking up and down and he said, 'It's good to see you Reverend, it's always good to see you.'

''And I said, 'Don't talk now brother Herron, don't talk,' seeing he was gasping for breath, and we walked slowly up and down till he got his breath and then we began to question each other like the fishermen on the sea of Galilee and we refreshed our spirits, talking back and forth, not agreeing, you understand, but giving and taking like brothers, coming to an understanding, walking back and forth and people came out of their houses, or walked along to speak to us, to say howdy, to overhear some of the

problems we were threshing out and it did everyone good,
always did, yes, he was health, you felt good and you had
to see him so often, you did, and it brought you health and
all our people health. . . . Many's the time in a fight I've
felt his hand on my shoulder, and you were glad. Yes, this
was a man of a new kind, in this place, in this time. On this
earth. Let us pray.''

We passed to look down again at that great, black
eroded face, so fierce, so full of tenderness, and his high
brow like a field of black earth he dug himself, gleaned,
hoed, winnowed, harvested with the great and only tool he
had, given him by the Party, the tool of Marxism. History
written on it as upon a map, of the past and a campaign for
the future, and all the passion and love and sorrow and
anger he taught us to feel, and now the ferocious leonine
death, crying havoc to all the conspiracies of power.

I ran back to get the rose for my friend from the spray
— and there on the fresh grave is the naked broken stems
of the wreath. Not a red rose is left from the wreath from
the Communist Party of Minnesota.

The Dark of the Time

Does the eagle know what is in the pit?
or will you ask the mole?
— William Blake

Our people in America are in deep anguish. They are in the dark of Capitalism. The assassin passes through your hands daily as the product you make passes into the chaos of a market you never know. The people suffer under capitalism in a different way than a colonial people, for the masks are cunning and the naked wars of aggression are hidden under the words of democracy, and you are delivered into the death of wars against people you do not hate, and made guilty by Nagasakis and Hiroshimas you did not plan.

An abyss seems to have opened between the intellectual cosmopolites of culture and the people, hungry for word and meaning. In the city you hear the words of contempt for our people. You even hear that our people have so many "things" — so many televisions, bathrooms, etc. Returning to the hinterland, I told this to a man who travels the Dakotas and he laughed bitterly. "The thing about capitalist 'things,' commodities, is that they are not permanent. They are an illusion, you never have them — not even the toilet — now in one whole section of Dakota the outhouse has returned — not that it ever left the majority of farmhouses — but now it is gone! The killing of the REA has thrown a whole community back to oil lamps, hand milking, outhouses! Everybody knows you never own anything under capitalism — it passes through your hands and one month's backpayment on the installment and whisk — it is gone . . . gone with the mortgage!"

Hurt myself by the "big city" mechanical "idea" of America, the pawn-moving feeling of some organization, I took a bus and fell down the dark flux of all on the move, the young reluctant warriors, in the stinking stations of the poor, the young mothers again following, Negro and white mothers with the hanging pelvis, the torn feet, the swollen veins, all night with the children swarming upon them, like all of us on the dark, gutted, eroded American earth outside the windows; and fragrant strong as that earth and as beautiful.

Wounded from the city, return — return to the dust of earth, to the angry lean men and the risen dust of wrecked men and women, descend among the gentle, waiters, movers; the angry boys, green down on their lips, going to far bases they hate; the young prostitutes clubbed by the billies of southern cops; workers going to other plants; a generation in anxiety moving to the burst of birth; old members of the Wilson brigade, of the first world war, half dead and crazy; dry-leaf bitter faces of the lost and damned from depression and war, mute and terrible testimony to the splendid "working of capitalism"; peddlers of every shoddy lust, living off the good body like maggots and lice, and all moving underneath, all is anguish and moving and the great culture of the underground common to our people emerging in the night like rich herbal emanations.

2

After I had slept, looking out at the hills and the moon riding over and the warm sense of people like myself, we stopped at a small village and a mother got on with a young child and two older ones, a boy of seventeen maybe and a girl heavily rouged and pockmarked. The mother and the little girl took the seat in front of me and the child looked out the window at the village as we pulled out and I could see the tear magnifying the eye for the leaving of the familiar village, for the journey and the joy of seeing her father who was on a construction job in Chicago and whom, with a fine contempt for space, they were going to visit. Nancy Hanks I am sure had a body like this, ill nourished, thin yet strong, gaunt, a little tall, black hair, blue snapping eyes, the weight and burden strained through a sharp militant humor. She drew the child down to sleep, with utter warm authority, gentle, no coercion, anger or tension. I could see her large knotted hand bear the child down.

She told me later she had ten girls and two boys, five at home, yet she was glad — a very good life. Work is good, a very good life with hard work, it is good not to have enough. You have to scratch. We get by. Her body was like a great poem to read. She gave it without stint, like the fields, fragrant, bearing you up, and the gentle emanation of forgiveness from her, of strength, a curious signal of resistance organized in her eyes.

I returned to the haven of woman, land, the great beloved woman of my country.

3

In the long night, plunging south, a land unfamiliar to me, but whose aroma rises to my nostrils, whose people, invasion thin, drift out of the night into the bus, alight in wide lonely landscapes, or little lanes dark under the trees, and disappear taking some of me with them, a crying ghost following their asking as they turn at the bus gate . . . I hear behind me two boys I have not seen, their voices light and terrible, emitting words of horror — one is going to Cincinnati on a book deal, forty-five a week and expenses for two weeks, he doesn't intend to sell any books, after two weeks he will skip, got the job by shining up to the boss's wife, could have had her too but he's already running from one alimony and an angry gal whose car he stole and all he wants is to keep running.

The other one is a sailor and says he would like just a plain old job. Nothing in a job, the other one says, you can work all your life and where are you? I done everything, from driving a cattle truck to a racket in Tammany. Nothin' in it. Make a haul, that's the only hope. Some kind of a haul. I'll make mine yet. The sailor says, the only thing I care about is a sweet fast car. I don't give a hoot in hell for my life. I don't even know where I'm goin' now. Just takin' off without a parachute. I want to just ride fast and straight into hell. I don't want to take no one with me, understand? I respect the lives of other people. I'll never shoot anybody. I never said this before but I'll never see you again but it's the truth, I'll never shoot at anybody. But I don't give ten cents for my own life. Not one cent. Just like to drive straight and fast in one of these new babies, straight into hell!

4

I was never in Washington, D.C., before. I looked at it from the best vantage point, from midnight, way down below, seen by mole, bat and night owl, in rendezvous with those who have something to say, who do not speak on the podium or broadcast, or who even try for the sixty-four dollar question or are queen for a day. Besides, after midnight there is no chance for any of this — Colgate's is not going to call your number, or the mail man bring you a message showing you are chosen from the nation to represent what? After midnight it is all over, so I was sitting in the lysol-smelling bus station, the small rest room

marked "Colored," and the awful smell of antiseptic that
permeates all official buildings.

I went downstairs, and outside the rest rooms there
were eight telephone booths, four on each side, and from
each booth there stuck out a pair of worker's legs, in work
shoes bent and battered, and from the booths there came a
strange talk. I had to listen a long time to catch any of it.
They were all Negroes come to this rendezvous after work
in the late night, or early morning. I saw no face, only the
battered shoes, one white from concrete, broken battered
feet of workers who work on their feet. I listened amazed,
there was much laughter but no face appeared. The feet
crossed or uncrossed. Someone was telling a story but it
was stopped by a kind of choral laughter and repetition.
It's as if they were slightly distended in the mouth into a
beautiful rhythm, the rhythm I could hear but the words
must be caught in the net of the beauty of the voice and this
gentle chant, and reiteration of the theme on a chorale of
laughter. I could see the huge brown and black hands
resting on the high knobbed knees. I could not stand there
and watch. There was a bench in the rest room where I
could hear the strange speech. It went on rising obviously
to some climax. I could catch a word here and there, the
farmer . . . stealin' . . . yes sir he was sore put — and then
at the end the whole was suddenly revealed and I felt a rich
delight suddenly as if I could run in and speak to all of
them for the teller on a whiff of laughter, a pouf of
laughter, said quite distinctly: "And then Br'r Rabbit said
to the bossman — do what you like boss man, do anything
you like, but don't don't don't throw me in the briar
patch. . . ." And on a great descending He! he! he! the
laughter joined, flew like sharp birds, the feet pounded,
hands clapped. . . .

The cop descended upon them with gruff voice, drove
them out. I could hear them walking out and I had the
feeling I would find the booths full of dead clubbed birds.

5

Upon the earth through the vent of the cities, the
people move in the dark of the American time. It is like a
descent into the South through the Virginia mountains,
where we see no town for a day and a sign says, Nancy
Hanks was born behind that spur of mountain, and we
glide into the deep tall night, into the brawny calloused
hand of our mother, into her herbal, rank and strong

odors. Like the mother of twelve she leans over us, covers us, her hair of night falling over our burnt asphalt faces.

At Louisville we descended into hell. It is one a.m. and Friday night and hundreds of soldiers are trying to get back to Fort Knox. The segregated rest room is one-fifth the size of the white. It is full of soldiers, also women and children.

The large area of a lunch room is full of soldiers trying to sober up on black coffee, or trying to get another bottle from the many old men and sharpers who are bootlegging bottles at three times their price. Small fights spring up. Old men slither on the stools beside the soldiers making deals, offering them anything from heroin, girls, to a ticket for the Kentucky Derby. More circumspect bookies circulate offering sure bets, talking into the ears of the sleepy dazed soldiers. No one is allowed to sleep. The civil police come along and punch them brutally — wake up bud. . . . For professional sleepers. Old men come in to get warm. The cops search their pockets, ask them to show a ticket, and having none they are plucked up by the nape of the neck and booted out. One worker becomes confused and cries to the cop — I have a job. I have worked all my life. I can't remember. I have a job, it's just the name. You don't work not for a man any longer — it is a company and I can't remember. . . . He was thrown out.

Above on a balcony the military police looked down upon the writhing mass, pointing out every beggar below, or sleeper. There were Negro and White MP's. They came down swiftly at any ruckus and used their clubs, they were armed with every kind of weapon.

I bought a ticket for Elizabethtown, Kentucky, where Nancy Hanks gave birth to Abe Lincoln. The turmoil of the station had come to a boil. A young Negro, very severe, sat bolt upright, and a peddler of bets for the Derby, a slick thimble rig, with the sharp face of the devil himself, stood behind him, set upon him, and a crowd had gathered as he baited him. A man's a man I always say, the pitchman said — it makes no difference to me what color a man is. He winked hugely, there was laughter. Leave him alone, a white soldier said, and swore at him roundly. He kept on — my best friends — still and all — there's a place for everyone, keep their places. The Negro soldier whirled, but before he could strike, the swift movement of many people out of a prepared coil sprang at the same time to hold him back, to snatch the peddler and move him towards the door and from the balcony came the running feet of the MP's, Negro and white, who laid about them.

The poisonous boil burst with foul pus out of everyone. The sound of the police wagon, the shouts of the people in the station, the defense of the Negro soldier, the drunken curses now of the peddler, his foul racism loosed naked, as the police half jerked his clothes off, lifted him, and, along with others, threw him into the wagon. . . . The Negro soldier was taken off to the military. The bus was now stirred like a foul slimy pool, violence broke out, people became sick, the girls shouted and tried to pull soldiers with them and then the bus came and everyone was herded into it and with a jerk we started south toward Fort Knox and Elizabethtown. . . .

It took an hour to unload the buses, some had to be carried out, others cajoled to return, some were weeping. They were so young. The bus driver, a young tender fellow, helped them all, gave them fantasies to live on, held them up, whispered in their ears, slapped them on the back. The last one gave me a big wink . . . goodbye, he said, we go to save the world! He stumbled and skidded for his balance, turned and made a derisive jesture, half despair, half in satire of himself.

6

I was going to Elizabethtown in the dawn and I was startled deeply for the earth was red, gashed, as if steeped in blood, man-red in the dawn that flooded the tipped spring moon which seemed to pour a blood light over us. I remember I heard the earth was red here but it is startling to see it, red earth out of which came Abe, from the red dawn of Nancy Hanks too.

It was before seven when I got to a tiny bus station at Elizabethtown. There was a taxi driver who had a Yankee accent. He told me Lincoln Park and Sinking Springs were about ten miles away. I walked down the village, around the square and the court house in the center of the square, a big house probably Tom Lincoln worked on, the cemetery spreading back on the hill.

It wasn't seven yet. I stopped in the morning restaurant where workers got their lunches and had breakfast. It was full of men. There was a young girl, a young

boy at the counter and a Negro woman doing the cooking
back in the kitchen. Do you know anything about Nancy
Hanks? I asked the young girl who was half crazy with all
the young construction workers ribbing her and eyeing her.
I don't think she lives here, she said. I just about know
everybody here. She shouted to the Negro woman — You
know Nancy Hanks? No, she shouted back. I said, she
was Abraham Lincoln's mother. There was a silence. No
one laughed. The boy said. She's daid. Yes, she is, I said.
He said after awhile — Say, on the corner of the bank there
is a thing there written about how Nancy Hanks got married to Tom Lincoln right there where the bank is.

I walked up there and sure enough it was so, a plaque
on the cornerstone of the bank. I went up to the cemetery
and talked to the grave digger, who knew everyone buried
there, and showed me the graves mostly of the merchants,
the bankers, the promoters. . . . He didn't see why he had
such a job, took a man's place seventeen years ago and still
at it, although the price of a grave had gone up consider-
able. The children began to go to school. I watched the
Negro children go one way and the white children another.
I said — how soon will the desegregation be here? He
shouted — Never. He said Elizabethtown had so many of
those bastards now since the fort and construction work
and there was no place for them and they would never have
it. He was very cold and practically drove me out of the
grave and disappeared, throwing up the dirt angrily.

I went out into the street now coming alive and I asked
a number of people and they all clammed up and looked at
me coldly. By the time I got back to the square a car was
following me. And as I walked, in every window faces followed me and I felt a terrible animosity. I had no way of
getting out of town.

I went back to the bus station and got the Yankee taxi
driver to drive me out to Sinking Springs. The country
looked very very poor, scraggly scrub stands, little poor
farms, thickets, the earth red. There is a park well kept
and on the high hill above Sinking Springs. The spring is,
as it was then, amazingly, a Greek temple with wide steps
going up to the pillars and supporting architecture of a Eu-
ropean world, and inside, guarded, within the foreign
marble, stands the original log cabin where, in the small
corner, Nancy Hanks gave birth to Abraham Lincoln.

No word is made of her. There is the door and the
leather hinge, and the fireplace and the wood glowing, the

same logs, the helve of the axe showing in the wood, from the energy of Tom Lincoln, and the half-open door seems to beckon you into the bare small rectangle, within the seed shadow, the hearth, fire, the door entrance, exit, wood and womb.

But here the woman unnamed, the cabin of her agony within the edifice of governing man, the thoughts of sages, all male, engraved around the solemn marble; around the wild unknown woman, hidden in the thought of man, bitted within an old dead idea, yet wild and strong she is yet in the body of all women. As I run down the steps I can see Sinking Springs just as it was, still discharging from the cave wall, still emerging fresh from the bought world, cold and fresh from underground. I put my hand in the deep water from deep down.

7

When I came across Kansas City to the crack train going north I felt I had entered another country. The clean, fat, groomed people had just gotten off the California special train from their vacations in winter; their faces bore another history and they were very annoyed because for some reason the train was an hour late. It was hot, the dust storms were standing below us in the sky covering Iowa, Kansas. They had come through it, and now the dust stood in the air like a venomed ghost. They were angry, for we did not know till later why the train was late.

The train is full of young hot soldiers returning home for their last furlough before going — where? They do not know. Many of them have slept in the depot. Some have not slept. A young blond boy sits beside me and he sleeps instantly, his fair face flushed, his big paws crossed over his loins and his long head falls on my shoulder. I timidly stroke his cheek. He seems hardly older than my grandson David and the same coloring.

For some reason there is no way to cool the train. It is unbearably hot. My soldier woke with blue eyes like David's, his cropped poll and red mouth, and he wanted to know why it was so hot and fell instantly into sleep again. I lay his head gently on the pillow and manage to get by his incredible mileage of long sleeping legs to the rear of the car where the soldiers have opened the half window in the vestibule and brought out the rest room chairs. I do not know then why the conductor is so tender to them, allows them privileges, looks at them like a grieving father.

It was the middle of the flushed hot afternoon, with the Iowa corn half a foot green, the tender light on the fields. The train stopped at a small town. It was the complaint of the tourists that the train was supposed to be a through train but it kept stopping. Only those standing in the vestibule leaning out of the half window saw why. The train had stopped, and in the midst of our joking we suddenly saw a young woman, her golden hair in a pony tail, run by, but her face was anguished, her mouth open as if screaming. We leaned out to see towards what she was running . . . and we saw four workers lifting a coffin from the baggage car to the waiting hearse and some friends held the young woman, whose eyes seemed distended, and in our eyes was reflected a coffin. One of the soldiers has dropped his hand on my shoulder and it is gripped hard. Korea! he says. Another boy begins to curse.

The train moves on. A woman comes out fanning herself — what makes the train stop? I paid for a ticket on the fast train. They'll hear from me! The boys are silent. She goes back. Now they pass around a bottle. When the train stops they are silent, when it starts they talk too loud. We are catching up on time, another woman says. Oh yes, the cursing one says, don't lose any time, get all the time you pay for. May they choke on their own fat! he curses.

We count how often the train stops — each stop a coffin, running crying women, the afternoon darkens for us. The boy is still sleeping. He might be the boy in the casket. So long, so heavy in sleep bolt upright, so beautiful. Inside the coffin the rot they have returned, the torn loins of the builders, planters, begetters. In our nostrils the dust of the afternoon, our agony, led into slaughters we do not dream, misled by leaders, our constant blind struggle, receiving the new dead sons quietly, revenge born between our teeth.

We are nearing St. Paul. The last stop, the swearing soldier leaned out and screamed — don't open it, for God's sake, don't open it, don't expect to find him there! We all hold him. He becomes very quiet, stands with his back to us looking out the window. We go along the deep mother valley of the Mississippi. One of the soldiers says, Boy, it's Saturday night. They'll be whoopin' it up on Seven Corners, roll back earth and take me home. This is Saturday night. Maybe the last, so let 'er go! let 'er go! The other soldier says — home! return, return he says,

there's where we went on Sunday for a picnic, the fishing
hole, the orchards, the prairies, the haying . . . the green
corn knee-high by Fourth of July. Oh God's country this
is, let me return. . . . Bring me back, that's all I ask. Receive me, furrow. Plow deep for me, Indian valley, bring
me home around the world. Oh! he cries, this country! Oh
my country. There ain't nothin' better, look at that river,
the crappies, the bull heads, Oh let me come back to you,
roll me back earth, around the world, roll me backward
earth and roll me home!

He keeps his face to the darkening land for he is
crying.

At the station in St. Paul a hearse is waiting.

8

Let us all return.

It is the people who give birth to us, to all culture, who
by their labors create all material and spiritual values.

No art can develop until it penetrates deeply into the
life of the people.

The source of American culture lies in the historic
movement of our people, and the artist must become voice,
messenger, awakener, sparking the inflammable silence,
reflecting back the courage and the beauty. He must
return really to the people, partisan and alive, with
warmth, abundance, excess, confidence, without reserva-
tions, or cold and merely reasonable bread, or craftiness,
writing one thing, believing another, the superior person,
even superior in theoretic knowledge, an ideological giant,
but bereft of heart and humility.

Capitalism is a world of ruins really, junk piles of
machines, men, women, bowls of dust, floods, erosions,
masks to cover rapacity and in this sling and wound the
people carry their young, in the shades of their grief, in the
thin shadow of their hunger, hope and crops in their
hands, in the dark of the machine, only they have the
future in their hands.

Only they.

The Return of Lazarus

with Elmer Borman

I looked at Elmer's face with deep anxiety as he leaned out of the window of the car and asked, "Which curve was it now? Sixty years is a long time and my brother is buried. Is it early for the crocuses to come up Melker Hill? There! There!" he cries, and his lean wood-carved Scandinavian face is sharpened by the winter wind from the old glacial terrain, from the frozen Mississippi that widens here at Lake Pepin before it travels on down to the sea. "There, that's Bogus Creek or is it? There the trout would be biting and my brother and I laid on our stomachs dropping the bait down where we could see the fish as clear as day. It was here — here — no this is not it, this is full of hazel bush, the forest is gone. Here there was a birchwood coulee. Gone . . . gone now. The village should be below, around this bend."

I am filled with love and anxiety for him returning now to his birthplace, and even the old limestone cliffs look like old men squatting as time roars across the shining lake. Even the air is wreckage above us, and we are sniped and shot in the back by ghosts and intentions that haunt us like old orchards, unbloomed. As we drop to the river's edge the village seems a carcass shape, a skeleton marking the flesh of men's intentions, and the abyss between flesh and ruin. I could see the gaunt thought adown his cheeks heated with anger and memory now and his blue sea eyes moistened to see the village of his youth so forlorn, a ruin.

The old river town, a skeleton, lay on the ancient beach behind the "Jim Hill" railroad tracks and the station marked nostalgically "Stockholm." Elmer got out and started past the station, looking back up the hill at the empty village to the farmed-out prairie above the cliffs, wheat gone, people gone. He started to run toward the big lake and the ice fishermen sitting dark in the great light and I after him, running through the sand over beer cans, dead trees, stinking fish.

"Look! Look!" He whirled in the cold light, like a ghost himself, twirling in some fierce vengeance and anger pointing like Isaiah up the bluff to the prairie edge rimmed by cedars. "That was the richest land, humus six feet

deep. We came and plowed it and thought nothing of it
and then we went on and plowed North Dakota and
thought nothing of it. I left here from that very station, on
an immigrant train, a lean lanky youth with land dreams
on a 'Jim Hill' excursion, so crowded we took turns to sit
down, crowded with land dreamers, athinking we were
going to a free homestead in a new state, a hundred and
sixty acres for all. What came of it all? What? What?''

His black arms fan in madness and grief, his coat falls
about him windless, the forsaken and ruined village reflected on his face, Ahab after the white whale. Who
ruined him? Who took his life and the life of the others? A
man can be cut down like a forest, can be ruined like the
earth — eroded, wasted — but as in the earth dread
forsaken fire burns underground and like the swamp fire
can be seen in the night of the soul and in the vengeance of
the body.

I can feel his thought in his face like the knot in wood
showing an injury. . . . (O let the house where I was born
be there. Let my dead mother and sister be there under the
cucumber vines and the great pines I planted. Here there
was a tiny spring where my brother and I lay, boys, dreaming of something that didn't happen. Yes, the tiny spring
circled the hillside and came out into a moss-covered
barrel, a rusty tin cup tied to it. From this we drank. The
water was so clear you could read a paper from the bottom
but we did not read the truth there. We looked west to the
land opening up. Now he is dead. I am old and the cool
cool water is gone . . . gone. . . .)

"Opening up," he said aloud, "everything was
opening up. There's the very station, see, it says
'Stockholm.' The immigrant trains went through night
and day. What became of all those people? Oh ho I was a
young feller then. We loaded my brother's machinery,
four horses, three cows on a freight car right there in the
night and food for the journey. We stood here by this very
cottonwood waving, right here, and he left for the new
land. We buried him last month with no land. I am an old
man and I have nothing. Nothing we have. Nothing.
Gone, gone, all is gone."

We look up at the forsaken village, the ghosts at our
back in the cold wind, the limestone of ages holding up the
richest prairies of the earth. . . . "And from here," Elmer
says, and I put my hand on his arm, "used to be shipped
the most barley and wheat, one of the biggest shipping

centers of wheat in the world. Would you believe it?'' He
is stumbling towards the tiny main street and the tavern.
"Hundreds of people with hopes lived here. There in the
river stone building the blacksmith kept a fire, there the
speculator in wheat, there the harness shop. Gone, the
town is gone.''

He turns and takes off his hat, baring the delicate fine
head of a woodworker, of a careful, necessitous and tho-
rough thinker. "Where have they gone?'' he cries into the
sharp teeth of the cadaver wind. "Where in heaven's name
have they gone?''

2

It was with fear we went into the dark Sunday tavern.
In the odorous gloom I was afraid the tavern keeper would
not remember Elmer. He was a little pale man with a white
cloth over his arm. A fisherman with a long burnt nose
like a turkish slipper hung his huge head around the booth
to look at us, bugled his scimitar nose, and spit clear to the
spittoon by the counter. He was in great need of the beer
which he could not get till church was out. I sat in the dark
booth hating to see Elmer's anguish. He must be
remembered by someone.

He leaned over the counter, down to the short man,
thrusting his lean face as if by force into his sluggish memory. "Why, don't you know me? Don't you remember my
two brothers, one, the wild one? Why, you were with him
right along. Remember the time the wild one took over the
bar, the bar right here, and the beer flowed right out the
door that night.''

The little man slowly wipes off the counter. Memory
seems like a fox he is watching approach cautiously and he
squints one eye to get a bead on it. He shakes his head, and
Elmer begins to ask these men who have never left the
dying village to remember what seems eroded in their
minds. Like the rim of the wheel Elmer circles the hub,
those who have stayed in the center of disaster and borne it
in sleep. He tries to make them see in him the lines of the
boy, the past they have murdered. To every name calmly
they both shake their heads like dead raftsmen manning
the boat over the river Styx. . . . "Gone, gone, he's gone.
We laid them away. Passed on. Disappeared. Never
heard from him again. Gone. Gone. Don't know where.
I guess he was dead, they buried him! Just left. You'll
find him up on the hill pushing daisies. Found him dead in

his barn. Killed in the war I reckon. Went to the big city, never heard of him again!''

Exhausted, Elmer returns to me and the present, sinks into the dark of the booth opposite me, speaks to the two men who listen to me, to the ghosts that now stand between the winter light and the beery darkness. ''I had my first drink here. I went to get presents for my sister, a doll, she died that year, and a tool chest for my brother who died in February. I had three beers and I got on the ice coming back. I was falling down and I was a sight and you said, 'Come on in, I'll fix you up,' and your ma gave me some soup, remember?''

He shakes his small head and keeps wiping the bar as if slowly wiping out every vestige of memory in Elmer. Terror grips us both. The lost day smokes on the dirty summer glass, shines cold as the tablets of Moses. Elmer in the dark seems to smoke with his memories, gets up, paces the length of the tavern. . . . ''Can't buy beer till church is out. Old Jehovah is still here, Meridel, roaring from the hills, in the thunder, calling people to heaven, calling them from being mortal, being human. Remember old Truro,'' he says to nobody, but the two river men are watching from beneath their old lids. ''Every Saturday he got solemnly drunk just to show the Lord God Jehovah he had no power over Old Truro. He sat straight up driving his black horses, drunk or sober, his black beard to his belly button. Drive across the rocking ice.'' Elmer's face darkened, and the voice of old Truro came over the rocking ice with the heads of the damned sticking through the abyss, roaring and shouting. . . . (O Truro you hated the wrath of Jehovah, as I did, looking from the face of river rock of time and sin, pointing from the church steeple, howling from the thunder, from the rocking cracks of the break-up, Jehovah, swallower of little babies, of rafts and steamboats, sucking them straight to hell, all all to his smoking breast, children's feet thrust from his black beard. I heard you beneath the ice shouting obscenities at the bright young girls in the thicket of sin. Strike me down, you cried to Jehovah.)

Aloud he said, ''One Sunday he was found dead in his cutter. The horses had stood quiet all night and he was sitting upright, the reins in his hand. My mother said God struck him down. I thought it was the booze.''

The barkeeper raised his blind village eyes. 'I remember that,'' he said, ''it was God *and* booze.''

Elmer runs to the bar. "You do remember. You remember. Elmer Borman. There were the Sandbergs, Larsons, Carlsons. Remember? My grandfather was the Moravian minister, built the church. My father farmed the sixty right by the schoolhouse."

They smile, cunning, an antique memory curling their senile mouths. "O Borman," he says without excitement, "yes, your cussins still living back there, you know behind the church. The old man had a heart attack right at the plow last fall."

". . . back of the church," Elmer cries, "then they came back to the old place?"

"Yaaas," says the bugle-nosed fisherman, "cussins marrying. I always say, they come back and now he is a dead man. You can still phone him. There's the phone. Phone him."

"I'll call my cussins," he says, his hand shaking as he asks for the number, his face looking vague into time as he waits for a voice from the meadow above, through space, "they are still there, still there," he says. "Hello. Hello. Guess who." The bartender begins to wipe the bar, but his pale eyes are fastened on Elmer's face, and the old fisherman has come over leaning close for he is far out in death himself. "Yes," Elmer says, "we're right down here on Main Street." He does not say the tavern. He nods, then hangs up. "They are there still. They're going to the second service. We'll go and see where I was born. Where my mother and sister died. We will return."

He half runs out the door and I can see by the strange look of the two boatsmen of death that there is no house, that all is gone.

We will return.

3

We turn abruptly from the river, past the abutments called Point-no-Point, past the wooden houses still with New England uprightness and decorum, and the white steeple pointing, rotted and dilapidated, but to heaven. We lift through the thicket rising into the long prairie sunshine.

"It might seem funny to you, Meridel," Elmer is excited now rising on the old familiar road, "but many citizens of Stockholm got their beginning in that thicket! You can't imagine, Meridel," he said, as the long prairie stretched in the bright sun, stubbled, and every winter copse surrounding the house, barn, neat upright, "you can't imagine how it was for my grandfather and father to come from a little country like Sweden, and then see all this land. I saw it after them and followed it west and we set the steel plows in her and ruined her in one generation.

"I know every house, I have walked every inch. I have plowed most of her, helped clear her, walked the wooden plow, then the steel, then the big machines. — Turn here! Turn here! The house should be here. . . . Here."

We turned onto a dirt road. "There! There!" he cried as we came to a grove of shaggy Norwegian pine. "It was there! I planted those pines!" I turned right angles into the kind of entrance into a copse lovers make invisible to night patrols. There was nothing but wild dried cucumber vines hanging from the unleaved thickets, a gnarled low apple tree, the rotted foundation marking where a house and a barn had been seen over the prairies, marking where cities of thousands had once been.

"Gone . . . Gone," he cried, as if it had never never been. "Right there I was born, in a lean-to in 1886; in that space my mother and sister died and we carried them out. There was the barn. There. My uncle was the community carpenter and he built the barn. My father used to walk to the barn with his pipe when the sun was coming up over his own land and say, 'Isn't it beautiful?' And he'd recite poetry in Swedish that sounded good as I'd squat down listening."

He would not get out of the car. I could see him through the glass as in a coffin as I walked around among the black plum thickets and the little chickadees scolded at me. "Elmer, come out, come out!" I cried, but the wind blew and the windows were closed and I saw his anxious thin face huddled in the coat fearfully looking out. I began to shiver. I opened the door and got in beside him.

He seemed to be talking to himself. "We all worked day and night always. I can remember when I was knee high to a grasshopper working beside my mother before we got the binder. I threw the oats behind the reaper and my mother bound the sheaves by hand. I can see her hands." . . . (O hands of the dead murdered mother, take the cutting straw from the loose sheaf on the ground, divide in two parts, the grain down, grasp the straws with the left hand near the grain and take the one half of the straw with your hand and throw it under and over your

right hand. There, there you stand, the banded sheaves in
your arms. . . . O mother the hemorrhaging blood, and my
father holding me by the nape of the neck . . . there in that
space he closed the door and held me as she died of her
twelfth child. . . . It is the will of the Lord, he said. I hated
him and the Lord. He would not let me run down that
slope for the doctor. She will live or die, he said, it is the
will of the Lord, and she died, died from us, from my
brothers and sisters, and we buried her on the winter hill
where the crocuses come early . . . sea of fire and brim-
stone. . . . Oh these houses held the terror, terror it was.
Repent, repent, Babylon has fallen, has fallen!)

"There in that space she died," Elmer said, "and it
wasn't the will of the Lord. See that white house over
there, to the right, why that woman there had gangrene
and her leg rotted off and her husband put it in the coffin
to wait for the rest of the body. . . . What could alter the
will of God? My grandfather was right. He said, "You
didn't go to Jerusalem in a gilded chariot but like Christ on
a jackass.' The picnic grove is gone, the people are
gone. . . . Let's be gone. Those are the pines I planted. I
was twelve and there they are." The winter wind groans
and soughs through the green beards of the old pines.

I backed out of the forsaken place back past the
school house to the road. "What happened?" he mum-
bled now, not looking at the winter prairie. "We worked.
My dead brother worked all his life. Anyone could carry a
small pail worked from the time he could walk. My
brother and I would carry the sheaves together, the men
pitched down the bundles to us, held the bank knife and
grabbed the twine with the other, and pitched them into the
machine. The long beards crawled in your skin, your
fingers were raw and bled but you worked from can't see to
can't see. The neighbors' kids in harvesting came too and
slept in the hay lofts. Yes, we worked all the time, all our
life. My cussins have done nothing but work for the mortgage. I went to that school till I was thirteen. That's all the
schooling I got. You have to be careful all your life what
you learn. I've read many books and everything in books
is not true, you know that, Meridel. It has to come from
everything that you have been doing and all the machines
you have been working. In my life came the reaper, the
binder, the thresher. I have seen these things in my life
time. I have lost my land, everything. What I have is
understanding. It took me all my life. I had to be very

careful to get the true understanding of the worker and
farmer. You can get a lot of understanding. You have to
learn or it will go on.''

    Don't look back. Don't look back. I cried to myself,
as I felt the dirge of the empty cold corpse of their death
and the rotten eye sockets of defeat start after us from
every empty house and barn, and from the graveyard the
dead women rose in the frosty afternoon light crying, ''remember. . . . Remember. . . .''

                                   4

    "You see that field?" Elmer pointed his long finger
as we passed. "Many's the time I plowed that field. It
used to be barley. Now it looks like it's lying fallow. Can
you imagine how they felt when they came to this rich
land?   There were the Bormans, Sandbergs, Larsons,
Carlsons, the girl I might have married lived there. We lay
on the bluffs . . . suppose I had married and stayed here
like my cussins with the vengeful God, singing sad hymns
at the top of my lungs. . . . We will assemble in God. . . .
But this land made me dream and hunger after land, not
righteousness. I tell you there is nothing like it. . . . I left
here and went after my brother to Dakota and there I saw
the land unplowed for a million years stretching as far as I
could see without tree or stone. It was 1908 and I filed on
free land. I went by stage coach when the railroad ended.
Then I hired a team of broncos and made sixty miles the
first day and I saw my land. I couldn't sleep for fear I
wouldn't make it to the land office. I was 21, a citizen and
I was the owner of land. I walked over my land with a
good and bright vision. It looked good to me. I built my
shack. I had a latch on my door and a bed of straw and
buffalo chips to burn. I had no horses and no plow but I
had thirty-five dollars to hire my neighbor. I dug my own
well and found petrified fish and shells. The land had been
there a long time. I plowed it up and seeded my flax by
hand from a rigged sack hung from my neck. I wrangled
extra horses, worked for my neighbors, helped with calving
eighteen hours a day, and came back to look at my flax,
which came to my knees. It was beautiful. The next day a
black cloud came up. I jumped to the hay rick and hit for
my place and in ten minutes there was two inches of hail
and my grain lay flat on the ground.

    "I hit the harvest fields. I borrowed six hundred
dollars at 12 per cent interest. Bought four horses, a

breaking plow and a disc harrow. I was in the trap now. I had a mortgage and interest. Well, it takes a life time to learn.

"There. There. That's my cussins' big mortgaged barn. And the original log cabin is the base of their little house. There it is. There they've been all this time."

We turn into the muddy confused barnyard, full of dead machinery, the thicket with abandoned cars, old plows, the refuse of a life time. The little white board house is covered at the roots with tar paper and hay to keep the cold out, the winter door is black tar paper. Elmer knocks and lowers his head waiting till the door is opened to a small wren's face. "You remember me?"

"No," Elmer said, as if she were striking him with a whip. She came on at him. "Why not, Elmer?" "I lost it, the mortgage, drought, grasshoppers. You always lose."

"It's the will of God."

"Now don't rile me up," Elmer says, "you got the barn paid for? You only paying the interest, I know."

"It's true," the old farmer says sadly, his huge hands hanging helpless between his legs. "It's true."

"Now what are you getting for eggs?" Elmer is going to give a lesson in economics. "Now somebody is making all the money off your eggs. In the city we are paying twice as much as you are getting. Who's getting it?"

"My hens lays the biggest eggs around here."

"But you don't get the feed back."

"The eggs we get, I say, is the same but we pay twice as much as you get."

"Yes," she says, "the egg is the same, no more has been added to it. It is the same egg for twice the money. Herod," she says, "is running rampant in Babylon."

"Now you come by some truth," Elmer says.

We must go. The two cousins who look like the wood they have cut and handled all their life lean beautifully and solemnly together, their big work hands embracing for the last time. Modestly she holds out her veined big hand and their only affection is in a little bow. As we drive away we look back and see them at the fragile door of the wooden house, thrown up as if they had not lived in it seventy years and more. "O God," Elmer cries, "What has their life been! O my God!"

Now the hills look like Golgothas and the roads to Calvary, and the strange black sarcophagus at the cemetery like some shaman of terror, and I wait in the car watching him with true anguish as he runs among the graves black and alive, searching, then stopping at what must have said Mother, Sister, Father, Brother. He stood for a long time in the dark of the snow which seemed to keep to the brow of the hill with the dead, tall and gaunt. I could not look at him.

(What have you got to say, you dumb and silent hills? How many lone thunderers have demanded answers? What is written on your undecipherable sides? Is there any message? Howl, old Truro. Do not be silent like my mother. O brother, I told you to understand or it is nothing. Let us all drop dead if we should forget you, O Jerusalem. Let our right hands wither and stink if we do not raise them in your defense. Howl, old Truro, I hear you. I hear in the tall pine wind, I hear you, my mother.)

I did not look at his crying face. It was growing dark. . . . "They were fierce men, my fathers," he said to the dark. "Roaring they went into the dark. 'Man,' my grandfather said, 'is sitting in a manure spreader deep in the mire.' Ascend, ascend," he shouted, "let the filth fall from the fiery wheels of Mammon as you ascend."

But we descend into the ruined village. "Stop, stop," Elmer says. The fishermen are coming in for a beer, leaving their lines descending into the icy elements below, "One more beer. One more."

Time, space, memory release the talk in men like flavor out of old wine. Elmer scanned the faces of the fishermen who came for beer now church was over, but he kept on talking. "It is interesting," he said, "to think of the meaning of time. Time is events and how we have grown from them. It is not regulated by the clock but by people and what they need and what makes them grow. My family is dead. My cussins are dying and what have they had but toil and labor? This day is a painful day but I would not miss it, Meridel. It took me all my life to understand. It has taken too long. Now over the earth it is coming what I have dreamed and I am old. I am proud I had much to do with it. I am proudest of this — that I spoke to the people and they spoke to me and I was not like my cussins alone, alone.

"I had a hard time learning. The people who own the mortgages control what we know. People are thrown into prison for holding ideas contrary to the mortgage-holding class and dare speak out the truth to the people. That is my only possession. My dearest possession — Socialism.

Right here in that church I first heard the word. The preacher said it was of the devil and we must shun it like hell. I never heard the word before, so why did he have to speak it?

"I heard it again in Dakota. I told you about my first crop. After that I worked like a demon. I went crazy to be a big operator. I sharpened my plows at night. I got a new-fangled thresher, hired out, got more mortgages. That year, it's crazy to think of it. . . . If the weather had been good, I had so much land seeded, I might have become a capitalist; then I never would have understood the struggles of man. Well, I was saved. The crops burnt to a crisp. Maybe we did not die of despair because things happened quick. There was all these new inventions and there was Socialism. This new idea spread like wildfire. The first farmer I worked with carried a bunch of papers in his pocket. He gave me one — 'There is something,' he said, 'for someone who wanders in the dark.' It said *Appeal to Reason* on it and I saw the word Socialism, and thinking of the preacher, I threw it in the fire. The farmer looked at me when I told him and he said, 'You're not to be condemned, you are to be pitied!' "

"Well, the season kept coming on, no rain, no crops. I was working for the mortgage day and night. Another neighbor who was a miner asked me to eat with him and to my surprise he had a library of books and the first one I took was Ingersoll and the next one was Paine. He went back to the mining camp to earn money for his mortgage and he sent a box of books. They were by a man named Marx. By kerosene lamp that winter I read until three in the morning. I did not understand all I read. I began to distribute things myself. I would have a copy of Victor Berger's paper, the *Christian Socialist*, in one pocket and Le Sueur's *Iconoclast* in the other. I never spent a lonesome winter from then on. We had dances in the farmhouses, talked and danced in relays till morning, twenty-five cents, and the women brought the cake, the bachelors the sugar and music. We argued through the winter nights, drew together, a light kindled between us. At the spring lambing as we waited we looked into each others' faces by the camp fires warming ourselves together in the light of Socialism. In the shearing pens, the hay barns, in the fields, in the machine sheds we had meetings on Socialism. Ring the bell at the schoolhouse and have a meeting like your father used to do. We took turns sleeping and the rest arguing.

"Now can you believe this, Meridel, I was known as a man who would work day and night. I got another mortgage, got a gasoline driven tractor in 1912. We had the Non-Partisan League then. We got the power in the state in a way. Much happened. The war, the wheat pools. We started co-ops, even tried our own newspapers. Some men killed themselves when organizations failed, others like myself went on to the next organization, the next step, the next try.

"You wouldn't believe it, Meridel, but when I lost my land, walked off it naked as a jay when the banker came, I tried again, yes, I did, I went to Canada, imagine that, got another mortgage and found it was the same there, till the depression showed us we had produced too much and got too little. I lost my land again, worked in a factory, a landless worker at last. I was talking Socialism and I was still able to believe that I would somehow be able to become a big operator under capitalism! I learned. That sounds like I was going to be a learned man, this is not the case. Perhaps you are tired of hearing about the mortgage. It is a very tiresome thing and my cussins are dying of it. Mortgages I maintain are not the American way of life. I am the American way of life. I am only one man who has a history. All people who create, make and have a history. If we could have a complete history of the people who have created wealth instead of the people who steal it, we would have a very interesting library of reading matter. Mortgages, you see, cannot live without people. We are the people. We plow and reap and build, and the joy I have had from the people! All those I had to meet talking Socialism. . . . They are the ones who learn from the facts of life. We are more nearly right all the time because it is the facts from which we come and learn. People have commenced to study this all out very seriously, even my poor cussin is beginning to ask 'where does it go the wealth I have produced?'

"Like Lazarus at the home of Dives, I have returned. I have returned many times to the tomb of my labor, Meridel. I went back to my beloved Dakota shack where I first thought I was a man of the land, there was a few strands of barbed wire, posts ready to fall, the remains of the foundation. My shack had died. Houses and land and earth die without man. It was an illusion. We were led into an illusion that we could have peace and security on a little piece of land and have a mortgage too. It was an impossible belief. You see here the ruin of a dead and wrong idea and you can read something greater than in any book. Facts are facts and these are the facts that in the end will make a new world and those that understand and take reality in their hands, they will be the most contented and leading people."

He rose, gaunt, and we went out into the dusk, his lean body straight with courage, his delicate stern head, and the strong life of his immortal hope.

As we drove back to the city where he lived in a furnished room he said, "I talk of myself because I am one of millions and it is important to understand me. It is the shame of my cussins, my dead mother and sister, of all our work going for nothing. There were those who gave us the illusion, lived on the men and women who sowed and reaped the golden grain, those who built the big mansions, took the money and went away and left us here with the earth eroded, suffering. We worked seven days a week, sixteen hours a day. Who robbed us? I did not even have to bother to sell my land. All I was asked to do was forget it. I will never forget it — or forget the labor of my mother.

"I found out and stood with the people."

We do not speak, but I feel near to him, and the earth does not reject us and the river flows for us, and in the old limestone of the earth and of man the underground fire burns, and we touch, and the hills as we move through them have an outward presence, a moving breast against our own, burning.